STAKES ARE HIGH

A DI KAREN HEATH CRIME NOVEL

JAY NADAL

PROLOGUE

AN AVALANCHE of thoughts crowd my mind as fear grips my soul and strips me of my power to think straight. I know there's no easy way out for me. He's made that clear already, and I've accepted my fate. He's beaten the fight out of me and told me what awaits me. I've cried a thousand tears and pleaded until my throat is red and sore. It's a sick business for him but one that feeds into his desire to see women defenceless, broken, and abused for the enjoyment of others.

Dying now promises an end to my agony, yet I mourn for the ones left behind, who will soon understand their grim fate upon hearing my screams.

When I asked him what we had done to deserve this, he remained silent, his face a mask of impenetrable ice, betraying not a flicker of emotion. Just his blinking eyes tell me that a human of some sort hides behind them.

Anger, confusion, and terror have come in waves. He must have got this wrong. We've done nothing to deserve this, and I'm convinced he's got us mixed up with others, but he's certain that's not the case.

I pray for my friends and only hope that their end comes quickly. Locked away in our own cells, I've not seen the others. Only heard their desperate cries. I've tried to talk to them. Whispered words of encouragement and hope. Promised that help would come soon. But we've paid a price for talking. He doesn't allow talking. He's already taken a tooth from each one of us as a punishment... and warning. My mouth feels swollen and the ache in my jaw pulsates like a dull drum. The bruises from the beatings have left me wincing in pain and too sore to move. He'll storm in and lash out for no reason at all, dragging me across the floor and pulling my hair up so I stare at the camera. Why? Is he recording it for his enjoyment?

He's watching me. I know he is. The little red blinking light on the camera hanging from the ceiling tells me he's stalking my every move. I'm so scared. I really am. I haven't wet myself like this since I was a little girl, and yet there's no mercy, little in the way of food and water, and no change of clothes.

He's outside. The rustling of plastic and the scraping of a chair or table as it's dragged across the floor reveal his movements. From somewhere beyond my door, a light turns on, and a halo of brightness frames my door. Please God, it can't be happening. I'm too young to die. What is he going to do to me? My body shivers with fear as my lungs crush my chest. As the minutes count down, I only hope that someone can save the others from what is about to happen to me.

The keys jangle and the lock turns. I squint and throw a hand over my face as the bright light pierces my eyeballs. He's framed in the doorway. A dark, towering silhouette with glaring arc lights behind him.

I don't have any tears left as he comes towards me.

I love you, Mum and Dad.

1

Two days later...

It was the call Karen hadn't wanted. The discovery of a body. A young, naked female. Karen stared out of the passenger window as Jade drove them to the scene. *It's calm and mystical out*, Karen thought as she watched the fields rush by. Evidence of the recent storm lay before her. Though the gusty wind had blown itself out overnight to nothing more than a chilly breeze, a web of moody dark clouds crawled across the sky, and morning mist raced through the trees and over the fields hugging low to the ground, masking her view in a ghostly grey.

She sighed as Jade talked to herself, relying on the satnav to guide her as they snaked through country lanes, every so often slowing to let a passing farm vehicle squeeze by.

"I hoped we'd find them," Jade remarked as she slowed at a junction. She looked both ways before pulling out.

"Yep, me too." Karen pulled the lid off her coffee cup and drained the last remnants of the cold liquid. She scrunched up her nose at the bitterness before placing the cup back in the cupholder.

Thirty-six hours had passed since the parents of three young women had reported them missing. Lifelong friends and keen outdoor enthusiasts, they'd gone on a three-day camping trip. The women often went off the radar for hours and sometimes days at a time, so it wasn't unusual. However, when all three hadn't answered their phones, it had raised an alarm, and police had initiated the search for them.

Her uniformed colleagues and officers had followed the usual procedures by conducting searches of their last known location. But it appeared as if they were too late.

Yearsley Woods was about forty minutes north of the city centre, but the journey felt like forever as Karen tapped her fingers on her door handle. The radios constantly buzzed with chatter as more resources were pulled into the area. Others from Karen's team were making their way there, too.

Karen knew they were getting close when she spotted signs for the woods. She felt a tingle in her chest. That same buzz appeared before every major investigation, especially when there was a body involved. Thoughts rushed through her mind. The extent of the injuries. The crime scene itself. What emotions and pain had the victim experienced in the last moments of their life? It was difficult for all those involved.

"Here we go." Jade slowed her car ahead of the roadblock.

Up ahead, Karen spotted the first signs of police activity with a police car positioned across the road, its blue light still flashing and an officer standing guard.

Karen pulled out her warrant card and opened her window as Jade stopped.

"Ma'am." The officer tipped his head.

"Where do we need to go?"

The officer stepped back. "It's about a hundred yards further up and round the bend. You can't miss it."

Karen thanked him before Jade pulled away. With the scene surrounded on either side by the woods, it felt as if the atmosphere had chilled a few degrees. She imagined how dark and menacing it would look in the middle of the night with a dark canopy of trees blocking out the moonlight. Jade slowed and stopped behind a row of marked police cars parked up on a muddy verge. Karen noticed a handful of white forensic services vans further up as well as an ambulance, which would be of little use to their victim now.

With winter on the doorstep, the chilly breeze whipped round them as they both stepped from the car. Karen's hair drifted across her face, masking her view for a few seconds before she wrapped the strands behind her ears.

"Looks like we need our wellies." Karen glanced down at the soft, wet earth and grimaced as she shook her head. She had never owned a pair of wellies before, thinking they looked ghastly. But having been in York for a while, she understood they were now an essential piece of kit, and something she had found to her cost when during her first murder enquiry, she had turned up at a location wearing shoes and then had traipsed through mud to reach the scene. The officers, concealing their smiles and laughter behind the collars of their high-vis jackets, had found it amusing.

Yearsley Woods appeared to have lost its vibrant soul. Apart from the conifers, most of the trees had shed their leaves, revealing their bony wooden skeletons that took on a life of their own, watching Karen's every move.

As they headed into the woods, officers were making their way back from the crime scene and pointed Karen in the right direction as she trudged through the undergrowth, feeling the soft crunch of leaves on the ground beneath her feet. They were a faded, shredded tapestry of autumn, filled with crisp, golden hues, deep reds, vibrant oranges, and pale yellows that blanketed the ground. It reminded her of the autumnal colours in the New England fall in the US.

"Jesus, we get all the glamorous locations." Jade sighed, trying to keep up with Karen as they moved on to softer ground. Their boots squelched in the mud, slowing their progress.

"Well, look on the bright side. At least we're out in the fresh air and not choking on the fumes of London."

Up ahead, Karen spotted the white forensic tent looming through the trees, and a larger police cordon in place marking the outer boundary of the crime scene. A scene guard acknowledged Karen and Jade as they approached, offering them both a pack of booties and gloves and asking them to sign in to the scene log. The forensic team had placed metal stepping plates in a line leading to the tent to keep the crime scene intact and reduce the risk of contamination or further disturbance to the ground. Muddy prints caught Karen's attention as they led off in different directions, indicating that they might have been left by the first responding officers, but some could potentially be attributed to the person or persons responsible.

Several forensic officers sat on silver cases documenting evidence outside of the tent, their identities obscured beneath white Tyvek suits.

"Okay to go in?" Karen asked.

One of the crime scene investigators glanced up and gave Karen a nod. "Izzy is inside."

Karen blew out her cheeks and steadied herself before pulling back the flap and stepping inside. Jade followed a few seconds later.

Arc lights brightly illuminated the tent in each corner to give the investigating team a better opportunity to capture both the scene and the evidence.

"Morning, Karen." Izzy sat back on her heels. Dressed in a white Tyvek suit, she knelt on a rubber pad, a pen in one hand and a clipboard in the other.

"Morning, Izzy."

Karen did her usual routine of studying the ground round the victim, and once happy with what she saw, turned her attention to the naked body, casting her eye up and down a few times before making her first assessment. A young, white woman, slim, in her early twenties, well nourished, with evidence of an external penetrative injury to her inner thigh and noticeable bruising to her abdomen, arms, and face. There were smaller flesh wounds and tears to her legs and abdomen. She'd seen similar wounds on victims left out in the open and were more than likely caused by foxes or other nocturnal animals. Karen pursed her lips and sighed, glancing at Jade.

Jade stood back with her hands stuffed in her coat pockets to keep warm. She narrowed her eyes in deep concentration as she stared at the body.

Karen stepped round to the other side of the victim and crouched down to inspect her face. "What have you found so far?"

Izzy pointed out the injury. "Quite a lot. It appears as if she died from severe blood loss. There's a deep knife wound just inside her left thigh. Looks like it severed the femoral artery."

"Any signs of a sexual assault?"

"None that I can see. I'll have a closer look when I conduct the post-mortem. Tomorrow work for you?"

Karen pointed at the eyelids that someone crudely stitched together. "Yep. And this?"

"Stating the obvious, someone stitched them together. Not a professional job by the way. I'm not sure why they needed to be stitched closed." Izzy raised a brow. "The poor woman suffered other injuries. They pulled out her teeth."

"Pulled out?" Jade stepped closer.

"Yep. Again, not professionally."

"Was that before or after she died?" Karen asked.

"My guess is before. I've had a quick look inside her mouth and there is a fair amount of tissue damage and coagulated blood."

"Shit. Torture?"

"I reckon. He really put her through the mill, and he tried to hide her identity by applying a corrosive liquid to the tips of her fingers and thumbs." Izzy lifted one of the victim's arms by the wrist and turned the hand over to show Karen. "The substance left deep burn marks and tissue damage. There's no possibility of retrieving fingerprints."

"Any other identifying marks?" Karen asked.

"Yes. A small tattoo on her right shoulder."

"A serpent, by any chance?"

Izzy nodded.

Karen closed her eyes for a second and offered a silent prayer. She had found one of the three women. Georgia Caraway.

2

Karen stepped out of the tent to get a breather and to gather her thoughts. Her eyes drifted off into the distance. Beyond the hive of police activity, the forest was deathly quiet, hiding the secrets of what it had witnessed. The bony trees looked on in mild curiosity, their branches bending into the scene to take a closer look. *If only they could talk.* Jade's appearance jogged her from her thoughts.

"Do you know what is so frustrating?" Jade said.

"What?" Karen replied with a shrug.

"That we couldn't get to her quick enough to save her."

"I know. I hate cases like this. Not only have we lost a life, but it's the heartbreak of informing her mum and dad. It's every parent's nightmare. No one wants to outlive their child." Though as officers, they had been trained to remain impartial and not allow emotions to cloud their thoughts or judgments, Karen's feeling towards the sick bastard who had done this was nothing but hatred. "What worries me now is where are the other two? Have they been dumped round these woods as well or are they somewhere else waiting to be discovered?"

"They might still be alive?" Jade said.

"That's the best outcome we can hope for at the moment. Can you arrange for a PolSA search and get a cadaver dog here to do a sweep in the immediate area?"

"Will do. It might be worth getting NPAS over here. They can do a heat source search in case the other two are still alive and are being held close by."

"Good shout, Jade. We are dealing with one sick individual. He didn't just kill her, but got a kick out of hurting her and inflicting the most amount of pain on her while she was still alive. Did he stitch her eyelids closed while she was still conscious to make her ordeal even more terrifying? Robbing her of one of her primary senses would only have amplified her pain further."

Jade didn't reply but tutted instead before reaching for her phone to call in extra resources.

Karen saw Belinda and Ty approaching. From the look on their faces, neither of them enjoyed having to traipse through the woods either. "Everything okay?"

"Yes," Ty replied, "though I look like an idiot in these." He stared down at his green wellies. "I didn't have a pair so borrowed them off another officer. The only problem is they are two sizes too big."

Karen stifled a laugh as she stared down at his feet. They looked like clowns' feet.

"I took a picture." Belinda held up her phone. "I'll show it to any woman he's chatting up. That should sink his chances." Belinda elbowed Ty in the ribs. "It will cost you lunch every day for the next month for me to delete this picture."

Ty smacked his lips and stormed off in a strop towards a huddle of officers close by, leaving Karen, Jade, and Belinda teasing him in his wake.

"What do you need me to do, Karen?" Belinda asked.

"Take a walk round the area and see if you can spot anything that has been discarded recently. The ground search won't happen until the resources are in place, so I don't want to wait in case there's crucial evidence out there linked to the victim. Her clothes, phone, a rucksack, coat, anything."

"On it." Belinda hurried off.

Jade stomped round on the spot to warm up. "Do you think the victim knew the perp, or are we looking at a stranger attack?"

"I don't know. If it's a stranger attack, then it's going to make the case even harder. He might have attacked Georgia and the other two, left them for dead, and left the county. If that's the case, he might be anywhere."

"Just as I left the tent, Izzy said that Georgia died in the last twelve to eighteen hours. So the killer has a bit of a head start on us."

"Who found her?" Karen asked.

"A rider on his mountain bike. He follows trails through the woods and spotted her not far off his track. Poor bloke is in shock. Officers took a statement and contact details from him before releasing him. I'll arrange for someone from the team to pop by and take a formal statement."

"Thanks, Jade. I need a bloody cup of tea. My toes are going cold. I guess the cold helps our crime scene because it's slowed down the rate of decomposition and preserved as much evidence as possible."

Karen fell silent when she saw three men in black suits making their way through the woods towards them. They were here to remove the body once the CSIs and Izzy had completed their work. Karen waved them on before turning to Jade. "No witnesses. No CCTV. No murder weapon. Not a great start."

"Karen!" Belinda shouted as she returned.

"What's up?" Karen walked towards Belinda to close the gap.

"About fifty yards beyond the tent is a wide dirt trail with plenty of tyre tracks. There's a set of tracks that takes a sharp right turn and stops a few yards inside the trees. It could be the spot where the killer parked and then carried the body further into the trees in the hope it wouldn't be discovered so quickly."

"Okay. Tape off the location. Speak to the CSIs and see if they can take some moulds. I don't think the killer had any intention of hiding the body. Look at the mounds of leaves on the floor. There's plenty there to cover the body, which would have meant she lay undiscovered for days and maybe weeks. He left Georgia on show for her to be discovered sooner rather than later. Either that, or he was in a hurry."

Belinda hurried off. It was already late afternoon and daylight was fading. The team had to work fast to capture as much evidence as they could before the woods plunged into total darkness. Karen made sure that enough resources were in place before she and Jade left. Although it wasn't ideal, they decided to postpone the PolSA search until first light the next morning, as darkness was just an hour or two away.

"Let's head back to the station and brief the late shift before calling it a day."

3

KAREN PUT the key in the door and stepped into Zac's house shortly after seven. Zac appeared in the kitchen and met her in the hallway as Karen kicked off her shoes and hung her coat up on the coat stand.

Zac wrapped his arms round Karen and pulled her in for a warm hug. "You must be shattered. I put your dinner in the oven. Shall I dish up for you?" Karen nodded, too tired to say anything. She stood in silence enjoying the embrace.

"What a shit day." Karen followed Zac into the kitchen.

Zac reached for a glass and got a cold bottle of wine out of the fridge, pouring Karen a glass and topping up his own. "Sorry about Georgia. Every bloody officer has been out looking for them and this is the news that none of us wanted to hear. Was it bad?"

Karen rubbed her temples as she flopped into a dining room chair. "Yes. Bad and bizarre." Karen sipped her wine and enjoyed the cold crisp taste before describing the scene.

Zac agreed with Karen's assessment of the killer being a twisted nutjob and he winced as Karen described the eyelids being stitched together. "Well, considering the remoteness of the crime scene, let's hope that Izzy has useful insights, and Bart's team recover some decent forensics for you."

Karen welcomed the hot bowl of meatballs with pasta. She had eaten nothing since lunchtime and being out in the cold had left her chilled to the bone and famished. "How's Summer?"

"She's upstairs watching something on Netflix."

"I'll pop in and see her before I go for a shower." Karen had a genuine fondness for Summer, and the more time she spent with her, the more she grew to love her. She was funny, and often on the same wavelength as Karen, which made it easy to wind up Zac.

Since the incident with the Harmans' associates, Summer had been having regular counselling sessions to come to terms with the traumatic event and the panic attacks and fear she felt, especially when she was on her own. Where possible, Zac had ensured that parents of Summer's friends would take her to and from school if he could not. Additionally, Zac installed extra tracking software on her phone with an emergency feature that would be triggered if Summer pressed and held the number one digit for three seconds.

Zac stood behind Karen and massaged her shoulders. Karen groaned in relief as the tightness in her shoulders melted away.

"Thanks, babes, I really needed that." Karen rolled her head from one shoulder to the other, the bones in her neck cracking in protest.

"Any news on Sally Connell?" Zac asked.

Zac kept bringing it up. Karen understood that he was

equally, if not more, worried than her. And it was totally understandable. He had already had a close shave with his daughter's safety because of the Harmans. If Sally Connell came after her, Karen knew that her relationship with Zac would put him and Summer at risk. Dealing with criminals always came with the risk of reprisals. It was why officers were always reminded to vary their routes to and from work, and to stay vigilant for anything unusual near their homes.

"Nothing yet. Laura keeps asking me how I am, and I know she's making enquiries on my behalf. I'm in York now. London isn't my patch. I'm sure she's keen to re-establish a foothold in London, but that's not my problem any more. She'll have enough on her plate with the authorities monitoring her every move, so I can't imagine her doing anything stupid." Karen really wanted to say that if she ever came across Sally Connell, she would wipe her off the face of the earth once and for all, but that wasn't something that Zac needed to know.

"Well, just be careful, okay? I don't want you getting hurt." Zac leant over Karen's shoulder and kissed her on the cheek. "I'll tidy up down here. Why don't you go upstairs and see Summer and grab a shower? I'll be up soon."

Karen pushed back in her chair and stood up. Every muscle in her body ached as if she had run a marathon. Maybe she was coming down with something, or perhaps standing in the cold wet woods had chilled her to her core. "Thanks for dinner." Karen gave Zac a long, lingering kiss before dragging her body upstairs. She was fast asleep by the time Zac came up.

4

Ripples of conversations floated round Karen as she took a place at the front of the SCU team and alongside a new whiteboard. She cast her eye round her officers and sensed the energy and keenness to get on as the volume of voices grew.

"Okay, team. Can I have your attention and let's get started." Karen placed a notepad and phone on a free table beside her. The conversations petered out as officers swivelled in their chairs in readiness. All eyes were on her as a hushed silence spread across the room.

"As you all are aware, the misper enquiry has become a misper *and* murder enquiry." Karen turned to face the whiteboard. She pinned images of three young women to it and wrote their names beneath each one. "Georgia Caraway, Raveena Chowdhury, and Louisa White. All aged twenty and from the Swansea area. Friends since reception class and now all at university."

Karen gave the team a few moments to study the photos. "Their parents describe them as bright, enthusiastic, independent, and intelligent young women with boundless energy, a sense of moral responsibility, and a willingness to help."

She paused at studied her team before continuing.

"Georgia is at Exeter, Raveena at Newcastle, and Louisa at Leeds. All three are keen outdoor enthusiasts and accomplished campers. They've done the whole Brownies and Guides thing and were in the middle of their Duke of Edinburgh's Award. According to their families they had been on many Girl Guide camps, and were used to, and comfortable with the outdoors."

"They sound like a wonderful bunch of girls. My daughter was in the Guides a few years ago," a female officer said softly, though her face did little to hide the pained expression in her eyes that any mum could relate to. Karen smiled back. Myriam was a support officer in Karen's team and a mum to three kids, her eldest daughter of the same age as Georgia and at university in Glasgow.

Karen took a moment to add a few extra notes to the whiteboard before she continued. "As you know, their parents couldn't contact any of them, which was unusual, so they initiated a missing person enquiry."

Jade, who was sitting close to the front, chipped in. "The parents were keen to contact them having heard about the recent storm and heavy rains that swept across the county."

Karen nodded in agreement. "The body discovered yesterday morning is that of Georgia Caraway. Swansea police brought her parents over late last night to identify her." Karen updated the team on the extent of Georgia's injuries and urged everyone to review the body cam footage from the first responders on the scene. "Dan, you met them at the morgue last night. Thanks."

Dan nodded. "They were in bits. It must have been an awful journey knowing the outcome. I had to look away at one point. Georgia's dad did his hardest to support his wife, but... Jesus, I've not seen a man cry like that before..." Dan swallowed hard as the words caught in his throat. He looked down at his notebook for a moment to compose himself.

"I'm sorry, Dan. It couldn't have been easy."

Dan shook his head and cleared his throat. "A FLO accompanied them, and DCI Owen Lewis from Swansea homicide. He needs you to call him when you get a moment. I've got his card."

"Will do. Thanks. I'll grab his details after we wrap up."

"Is it possible that Raveena and Louisa have come to harm as well?" Dan asked.

"We have to hope they are still alive; but time isn't on our side. We have a PolSA search team on site first thing today. A cadaver dog did a sweep last night but found nothing. They'll be back again this morning. I wanted it to start not long after we arrived, but conditions were heavy underfoot and it would have been difficult to find anything. NPAS didn't find any large heat sources yesterday evening. They noticed a few small ones, but they were moving too quickly, so were probably foxes or deer."

"Anything from the eyewitness?" Claire asked.

An officer from further back in the room piped up. "We visited him last night. He'd slowed down to take in water and spotted her. There were no other vehicles or people around at the time other than a female horse rider he'd seen ten minutes earlier. He's not seen her before."

"Okay, we need police notices put up appealing for witnesses." Karen added that to the board. "We also need to look for Raveena's twelve plate black Astra. As yet, we've not been able to locate it. Run another check through ANPR for me, Ty."

Ty nodded and made a note of it.

Karen turned to face her team. "I can't stress enough the importance of finding the other two women. But we don't know who we're dealing with. Was it a stranger that abducted them or was the killer known to them? And why Yearsley Woods?" Karen moved over towards the map on a second whiteboard. "As far as the parents were concerned, the women had chosen to set up camp in Kilburn Forest, six miles from where Georgia's body was discovered. What's the significance? We've already had teams on the ground searching Kilburn Forest and NPAS have done a heat sweep. So far nothing."

"Perhaps the killer was more familiar with Yearsley Woods and the surrounding area? Or it was on his way home? A route he takes often?" Belinda offered.

"It's a possibility." Karen drew a line between the two places on the map. "I couldn't see any personal possessions close to the scene, but then again, the woods are massive. We need to go back and extend the search area as the last cell site data for their phones is at odds with the information given to us by their parents. Phone signal is sketchy between Kilburn and Yearsley Woods anyway, so that could be one reason the parents could not reach their daughters."

"Karen, what's your take on Georgia's eyelids being stitched together? A ritual thing?" an officer asked.

"I'm not sure, is my honest answer. I spoke to Izzy about this. It could have been a part of the perp's torture or a very sick and twisted way of intensifying the fear and terror that Georgia experienced. I've not come across something like that, so this could be part of his MO. Can you contact the NCA and see if they've come across cases like this before? Perhaps it's a serial killer's signature mark?" Karen clicked her fingers together as she thought this through. "While you're at it, run a search on prisoner release records for the past twelve months. Has anyone done something like this before?"

"I've organised a press release with our press office," Jade said. "I'll email it to you for approval or amendment."

"Thanks, Jade." Karen picked up her pad and phone. "We'll reconvene later. In the meantime, I need you all to work hard and fast. This is a major investigation, and all eyes are on us. We need to work out their last known movements and where Raveena's car is. Jade, can you organise a team to search their bank records for any unusual withdrawals in the last twenty-four to forty-eight hours, their social media profiles, list of friends, exes, and call histories from their phone providers? Once you've sorted that out, we need to head to the PM."

Karen headed back to her office. The post-mortem was scheduled to begin in forty minutes, giving her some time to catch up on emails and grab a coffee.

5

_____

It was a mission that morning to find a parking space in the hospital car park. Karen drove up and down each aisle looking for a vacant space, but the only ones available were a few disabled spaces.

"It doesn't matter which hospital you go to, they never have enough parking spaces." Karen slapped her hand on the steering wheel in frustration.

"Pardon the pun, but they make a killing in parking fees," Jade added, craning her neck left and right to search out an empty spot.

"I think it's been a bone of contention with visitors for years now. Visitors receive a parking fine if they are late returning to their car. They shouldn't be blamed for being kept waiting for their appointment, or for their treatment taking longer than anticipated, or for being stuck in A & E with a wait time of four to five hours." Karen blew out her cheeks and then sped up hard when she saw a car pulling out further up. She slid into the spot and gave Jade a wink. "There's not even an NCP car park near here. I remember going to see a victim at the Princess Alexandra Hospital in

Harlow. Their car parks cost a fortune. And yet, I parked in the Water Gardens car park ten minutes away for half the price. Why don't more people do that?"

"Laziness I guess."

Karen and Jade headed for the entrance and dodged a few patients in their pyjamas hanging round the main doors having a sneaky fag. It was a short walk to the mortuary and once inside, they gowned up and headed for the main examination room. Karen heard the music and rolled her eyes as she pushed through the doors. *The Final Countdown* by Europe belted through the speakers of a small radio on the bench in one corner. Izzy didn't appear to be the typical headbanger as she nodded along to the song.

"Ah, there you are. Good to see you both," Izzy said in a tuneful way. She instructed her assistant to turn down the music.

"Sorry, parking was a bitch as usual." Karen and Jade took up their positions on the other side of the examination table. Izzy had already started her formal examination.

Karen took a moment to study Georgia's youthful and slender-looking body. She couldn't ignore the feral bite marks that peppered her skin. There were more than she had noticed at the crime scene. It was a sombre moment in Karen's opinion. The cold steel of the table, the cream tiles on the walls and floor, together with the fluorescent tubes of light, bleached the surroundings and only added to the chill Karen felt. A shiver raced down her spine.

Georgia Caraway looked peaceful where she lay, but it felt like such a waste of a life in Karen's opinion. She had so much to look forward to. Graduating from university. The start of a career. A relationship, and perhaps even a family. She would experience none of those things now. A life extinguished too quickly by an evil and sadistic monster. Even though she was gone, there was no dignity for her as Izzy prodded and poked her body looking for clues.

"You okay?" Izzy asked, catching Karen's thoughtful stare.

"Yep, I just feel so sorry for her and her family." Karen's chest tightened as an image of Summer's face replaced Georgia's on the table. It could have been Summer lying there if Harman had carried out his threats. Karen blinked hard to wash the image away from her mind. "What have you found so far?" Karen asked, needing to get back on track.

"A lot more than I expected. Cause of death was blood loss. She suffered a severed femoral artery, which would have caused her death within minutes."

"I guess that's a blessing of some sort," Jade said.

"Any sexual interference?" Karen asked.

Izzy shook ahead. "Nothing that I can see. There is no damage to her pubic region, vaginal cavity, or anal passage." Izzy continued. "As noted at the crime scene, the tips of her thumbs and fingers suffered severe burns from a corrosive substance. I've taken a skin sample to determine the substance used. She had little in her stomach. But her last meal was bread. Though there's no clothing to examine, I found a few clothing fibres on her skin which I will send off for analysis. I've also taken nail scrapings and there were grazes to her palms, heels, and elbows."

"From being dragged?"

Izzy shrugged a shoulder. "Most likely, Karen. There is bruising beneath her armpits and towards the top of the chest in line with that theory. But that's not the worst of it."

Karen braced herself. What other terrible atrocities could Georgia have experienced?

"Two significant points here. Her teeth were removed while she was still alive. We found coagulated blood in the throat and lungs. We also identified significant bruising and tissue damage to the inside cheeks of her mouth and gums, which suggests they were removed against her will. I would think she suffered a significant amount of pain and trauma. I've taken a blood sample in case there are any traces of anaesthetic, but I doubt it."

Karen rubbed her temples not wishing to believe Izzy. "Every single tooth?"

Izzy nodded.

Karen looked at Jade who offered nothing more than a shake of her head in disgust.

"Whoever did this tried their hardest to remove ways in which we could identify the victim, namely fingerprints and dental records. What he didn't bank on was the tattoo on her shoulder."

Threads had been removed from George's eyelids. "Anything unusual about the kind of thread used on her eyelids?" Karen asked as she leant in to take a closer look at Georgia's face.

"It's a thicker thread. Often used in heavier garments, maybe leather. Bart's team should be able to identify its composition. See this," Izzy stated.

Karen and Jade both gasped. They exchanged looks of confusion and horror. The killer had removed Georgia's eyeballs and then replaced them back to front, with torn muscle tissue and veins poking out towards Karen and Jade.

"What the fuck!" Karen shouted. "What the bloody hell has he done?"

"He gouged out her eyes, cut them off at the optic nerve, and replaced them. Why, I don't know."

Fearful of the answer, Karen was scared to ask the question. "Before or after she died?"

"Before." Izzy rested her hands on the steel table and bowed her head. There was nothing else she could say.

"Shit." Karen stepped away from the table, heart pounding in her chest, hands balled into fists, eyes fixed wide in anger. She gritted her teeth before slamming her hand down on the adjacent examination table. There were no words to describe the brutality. Her killer had a warped and unforgiving mind. "Why?" she muttered to no one in particular.

The three of them fell silent for a few moments, no one knowing what to say. Each one of them processed their own thoughts.

A few minutes passed before they reconvened at the table. Karen looked at Georgia's face. "I'm so sorry. You didn't deserve this."

"I feel sorry for the parents who are going to have to listen to the catalogue of injuries during the coroner's inquest," Jade remarked. She turned and headed for the door, unable to listen any further.

Izzy levelled her eyes at Karen. There was a coldness in her stare. "Make sure you find this bastard."

Karen pursed her lips and nodded before leaving.

6

BOTH KAREN and Jade were lost in their own thoughts on their way back to the station. For them, most post-mortems were a standard procedural thing they'd attended dozens of times in their careers, but this one hit a nerve which upset them. Whether it was Georgia's age, her innocence, and purity, or the barbaric acts committed on her, both women were consumed with a mixture of rage and deep sadness. Karen gripped the steering wheel all the way back, her knuckles white from the effort.

"You okay?" Karen asked as she pulled up in a parking space and stepped out of the car.

"I'm not sure what okay means these days. We see so much shit that ninety-nine per cent of the population never sees. Stuff that would make their stomachs turn, and yet we are supposed to act normal?"

"Jade, we're only human. It's natural for us to feel emotional amid tragedy. We just have to be good at managing it and remaining objective. There are friends, colleagues, and families out there who rely on us to bring the perpetrators to justice. I won't lie. I've come home after a hard day and cried. Sometimes I doubted if I could continue. But we are part of the thin blue line, which is becoming thinner by the day. If we do nothing about it, who will?" Karen put her arm over Jade's shoulder and gave her a gentle squeeze as they walked towards the building. "I know I'm your boss, but I'm also your mate. I care about you. If this shit ever becomes too much, you need to unload on me. You also need to remember that when you become a DI, your team will look for guidance from you."

She thanked Karen for the pep talk before they parted ways with Jade heading back to the team while Karen went in search of Detective Superintendent Laura Kelly.

Karen hovered outside Kelly's office waiting for her to finish with another officer before being called in.

"Karen. Have you got an update for me? The ACC was on the phone with me this morning. I'm sure it's not lost on you that this is a high-profile case, so we can't afford any slip-ups." Kelly placed her hands on her desk and leant back in her chair, casting her eye up and down Karen.

It made Karen's skin crawl when she did that. It was as if she was eyeing her up as a piece of meat. She still wasn't sure if her boss was gay. There were rumours she was. Kelly never publicly spoke about her private life, and she rarely stayed at official police functions longer than necessary. There was very little Karen knew about her boss, and that troubled her because she was never sure of Kelly's motives.

"Jade and I have just come back from the post-mortem on Georgia Caraway. Her killer inflicted terrible injuries on her while she was conscious. What I'm unsure of at the moment is his motive, and whether he did those things because he got a kick out of it, or whether it was torture or punishment."

The corner of Kelly's mouth curled down as she nodded. "Do you think the killer was known to Georgia?"

"That's something we need to identify. Our key priority now is to locate the other two young ladies."

"Are you hoping they are still alive?"

"I think we need to remain optimistic. There is nothing to suggest otherwise, but it's very early in our investigation." Karen took a few moments to update her on the active lines of enquiry being undertaken by her team to build a better picture of all three women. "This is turning into a big job, ma'am. We now have five police forces involved. Ourselves, Swansea, because all three came from there, and Exeter, Newcastle, and Leeds, because they were at university in those three cities."

"If they were spread across the country, it is unlikely that they would have a connection with their universities."

"Agreed, ma'am. I need to make sure I cover all bases. I've left a message for DCI Owen Lewis from Swansea police to call me back. When I called his number earlier, he was unavailable due to meetings. His officers are speaking to all three sets of parents and friends in the Swansea area, and officers from Exeter, Newcastle, and Leeds are in contact with friends and lecturers at the universities." Karen watched as Kelly fiddled with her nails, scraping dirt out from beneath one of them. *Is she even listening?* "If there's anything of interest thrown up by those local forces, we'll send our own officers to follow up as we need boots on the ground here."

Kelly nodded and sighed as if thoroughly bored with the conversation. "Any thoughts on a likely motive?"

"Your guess is as good as mine. If it's a stranger attack, then they were in the wrong place at the wrong time. I should know more as further intelligence comes in. The first press appeal didn't throw up anything useful. I think it would be a good idea to put out further appeals to jog people's memories."

"That's a good idea, Karen. I think it would be useful for us to have Georgia's parents brought over again so that we can do a fresh appeal with them involved."

"I will suggest that to DCI Lewis and have a conversation with him. Anything else?"

"No, that's it for the moment. Thanks, Karen."

KAREN IGNORED the niggles about Kelly and headed back to the SCU, stopping by the kitchen to rustle up a cup of coffee. Flagging, she needed the caffeine hit even though it wasn't lunchtime yet.

Karen weaved through the desks, stopping every so often to get an update from officers. Jade had already brought the team up to speed with the post-mortem findings. Information was thin on the ground. She stopped by the whiteboard and studied the fresh faces of all three young ladies smiling and posing for the camera. She struggled to look at Georgia's face. Each time she looked into her hazel eyes, the blooded mess of torn muscle tissue and veins replaced them on the back of bulging eyeballs.

"Life can be so bloody cruel," Karen muttered. All three were on the cusp of a significant birthday. They were perhaps already planning their twenty-first birthday celebrations. The time for family and friends to celebrate a wonderful milestone and the transition from university life to the start of their new careers. From what she had read so far, Georgia was studying medicine and had hoped to become a doctor one day.

Karen turned and faced her team. "I know this is asking a lot of you, but with the restrictions we have on overtime budgets, I can't force any of you to stay beyond your shifts, but if any of you can during this investigation, I'd appreciate it. We have to find Raveena and Louisa as soon as possible."

Many of her team nodded in agreement and felt they wanted to stay out of the need to save them.

Ty shouted from the back of the room. "Karen, we have contacted over one hundred and fifty people from their Facebook profiles already. It helped us to build a better picture of all three, but there's been nothing tangible to help us in this case. The other forces have the three universities. It won't be easy to speak to everyone, but they will put up notices in the student unions, canteens, and all other public places. An email from each university will hit every student's inbox in the next few hours."

"Brilliant. I don't envy the number of replies that their teams are going to have to deal with. Any student could be a suspect. For all we know one student may have had an infatuation with Georgia and followed her here but had no choice but to abduct all three of them to avoid any witnesses," Karen said, but admitted it was an extreme hypothesis, but still plausible.

Karen felt unnerved by the scale of this investigation, which involved one victim, two missing persons, and an unknown attacker, she left her team to it while she tried to contact DCI Lewis again.

7

THIS IS GOING BETTER than I imagined, the man thought. He had disposed of her body but chosen not to conceal it too much. He had never intended to hide her body where it wouldn't be found for a long time. Instead, he'd left her in a place where discovery would be easy.

The smell of death surrounded him as he stared at the plastic sheet on the floor. Splatters of blood peppered the plastic and reminded him of one of those abstract floor paintings that artists did where they randomly flicked paint from a brush to create something that they allegedly called art.

Here, it wasn't art. It represented the last moments of Georgia Caraway's life. He'd crudely extracted her teeth with a pair of pliers and tossed them across the floor like discarded cigarette butts. Her screams still echoed in his mind as she'd thrashed in the chair, desperate to get away. The more she fought the more he earned. The tearing of her flesh as each tooth came away excited him. The sense of power he felt was something he had never experienced before. After receiving coaching from an online contact in

Arizona, he'd decided to take the plunge when he'd seen the financial rewards, despite having watched such things online many times as a voyeur.

An overwhelming stench of urine and shit assaulted his nostrils. She had lost all control of her bodily functions as he'd destroyed her. And the more they'd bayed for her blood and eventual demise, the more torture he'd inflicted. But one of the requests online had really changed things for him. Someone had wanted her eyes removed while she was still alive, gouged out with a screwdriver and severed before being shoved back in back to front. Another request had taken the situation a step further, suggesting that her eyelid should be stitched back up, leaving an unpleasant surprise for whoever found her.

Pressing the knife deep into her thigh, witnessing her final moments, had burnt the memories into his brain. An involuntary reflex had tossed her head back. Damp, matted hair had clung to her face as blood had streamed from her mouth. She'd looked like a demented witch as she'd twitched before her head had dropped forward one final time.

He grabbed his cleaning cloths and disinfectant and cleaned down the chair in readiness for the next victim. Georgia's teeth and clothes would be gathered up and destroyed. The man rolled up the plastic sheet and left it by the door before returning to the laptop on the table close to the middle of the room. He wiggled the mouse and then two images appeared on the screen. Two live feeds, each showing a woman in her cell. He studied them for a minute. They were both pressed up into a corner, with their knees pulled into their chests. He smiled. They look terrified and so they should be. Though they hadn't seen what had happened to their friend, they had heard everything. Every cry, scream, and plea for him to stop. He remembered seeing the Asian one cowering in the corner with her hands over her ears sobbing uncontrollably, begging on behalf of her friend. Unfortunately for her she'd only made it worse for her friend as the donations grew.

Voting had started again minutes after Georgia's death with a flood of requests which made him smile. Removing Georgia's eyes had netted him sixty-five grand with one wealthy viewer from Saudi placing a fifteen grand bid. *Pocket change*, the man thought.

Adding sound to the video feed was a good shout, which amped up the excitement of those watching. It whipped them into a frenzy.

He grabbed his keys from the table and headed to the cells to check on the two women. The mere sound of his keys jingling was sufficient to make the Asian woman quickly move away from him across the dirty, chilly floor. She hid her bruised and swollen face behind her hands, not wanting to give him the chance to beat her round the face again or pull out more of her teeth as a punishment for being difficult.

"You stink and need a bath," he sniggered, staring at her crumpled form. He checked the bucket. "Empty. Not surprising as it smells like you've shit yourself." He tossed her a slice of white bread before leaving and locking the door. The second cell smelt just as bad with another empty bucket. "Personal hygiene isn't your strength either, hey?" He tossed another slice of bread towards the woman in the corner. She balled her hands into fists and tucked them up beneath her swollen chin. She too had lost a few teeth. A necessity in his opinion. As long as she remained compliant and quiet, he wouldn't pull any more. He took a moment to study her. She looked younger than the others, with a rounder face and chipmunk cheeks. Her long dark brown hair, once shiny and attractive, now clung to her clothes in a knotted and dirty mess. The dampness in her wide eyes shimmered in the light as she panted hard, the fear gripping her body that rooted her to the spot. "Enjoy the rest of your stay," he said as she whimpered in the corner. He would need to check on them later as he looked at the door and grabbed the plastic sheeting.

He didn't have a preference as to who would be next. That wasn't up to him, as moments later, he stood watching the plastic sheet, teeth, and Georgia's clothes being consumed in an orange and yellow glow of flames. Black spiralling plumes of acrid smoke pirouetted into the air, the smell catching the back of his throat. He coughed as he took a step back and threw a hand over his mouth. It would be a while until the flames consumed everything, but he needed to be sure to destroy every shred of evidence before he could leave.

I can't wait to do this again, he thought as he walked back to his van an hour later.

8

THE RICH, warm aroma of coffee wafted round the kitchen as Jade walked in. An earthy, nutty smell that made her groan in need of a caffeine hit. "Oh, my God, that smells good. Didn't make me one?"

Karen laughed and dangled an empty packet in front of her. "Sorry, I only had the one. I found it in a kitchen drawer at Zac's, so I took it."

"Typical. Think of yourself why don't you. I'll go to the canteen. Coming? Any joy with contacting the DCI in Swansea?"

Karen nodded and washed her spoon and left it on the drainer to dry before following Jade, mug in hand. "He's calling me back any minute. We seem to miss each other, but I've promised to leave my phone free."

The canteen was busy as usual. With the afternoon shift change, officers coming off the morning shift wound down and grabbed a bite to eat before heading home. Jade ordered a coffee and a doughnut before joining Karen, who had bagged a table in the corner away from the loud conversations going on round them.

"It's busier than usual." Jade glanced round.

"I think they had a big op on this morning," Karen replied. She reached across to pinch a bit of Jade's doughnut.

"Oi, get your own."

"I think it's only fair that you share with senior officers."

Jade recoiled in mock disbelief. "Oh, so it's like that, is it? Pulling rank on me now. You've changed!"

Karen loved the banter between them. Other than Zac, she regarded Jade as her closest friend. And even though she was her superior, it had never felt that way with her. Jade was easy-going, conscientious, and enjoyed a laugh. She could tell her anything in confidence, knowing that it wouldn't go any further.

They took a few moments to enjoy their coffees and sat in silence. Neither was in a hurry to say anything for a while.

Jade wiped the sugar from her lips and scrunched the napkin into a ball before tossing it on to the table. "What's your take on the case? My guess is it's a stranger abduction and killing. Wrong place and wrong time."

Karen placed her mug down and stared out of the window at the staff car park behind the building.

"I wish I knew. I'm still getting over the shock of the barbarity. There's no way he could have done this for the first time. Killers often grow into this kind of thing, starting with violent assaults, then abduction. Then they commit their first murder, and once their bravado and confidence grow, they commit worse atrocities."

Jade wasn't too sure. "The NCA haven't identified anyone fitting the bill. If there was a serial offender, they would have been flagged on their system. But they've got nothing for us."

"It could be someone who has come into the country. Maybe they committed similar offences in their own country and fled to the UK?"

"We're still checking with our European counterparts. It might be a few days before we hear."

"That's the problem, Jade. We don't have a few days. By then Raveena and Louisa could be in body bags too."

The grim prospect left both of them in silence as they considered that outcome.

"Hey, you two, I'm not interrupting, am I?"

Karen glanced over her shoulder to see DI Anita Rani standing there with a bottle of water in her hand. "Sorry, I was miles away. I think we both were." Karen looked at Jade. "You joining us, Anita?"

"I don't mind if I do." She pulled out a chair and sat alongside Karen. "How are you getting on with the new case? I know the pressure is on. I can lend you a few more bodies if you need them?"

"Cheers, Anita, I might take you up on that. I'm getting a bit of heat from upstairs. It's a challenging case. When we discovered the full extent of our victim's injuries, it rocked all of us. We can't let that happen to the other two that are still out there somewhere."

Anita nodded, understanding the impact.

"How are things on your side?" Karen asked, draining the last of her cold coffee.

"My team are dealing with a home invasion case gone wrong. A burglary that turned into a violent assault."

"That's not good. What are the details?"

Anita unscrewed the cap from her bottle of water and took a quick sip before continuing. "We have a wealthy couple in their sixties. The husband is fighting for his life after suffering a heart attack. They forced the couple, who were tied to chairs, to reveal where they kept their cash and jewellery. The house was turned over. When the husband refused to give in to their demands, they beat him black and blue, resulting in him going into cardiac arrest."

Karen tutted and looked in Jade's direction, who looked as appalled.

"We've got five of them on CCTV. The couple had no way of defending themselves. Since they live in a remote location with just a few houses on their street, it took a while before someone raised the alarm."

"Absolute scum. They knew that even if the couple had dialled 999, it would have taken us ages to reach them, and by that time they would already be far away," Karen said.

"Exactly."

Karen turned in her chair to look at Anita. "Is there anything we can do?"

"I know you're maxed out at the moment, but would you mind checking in with your team and asking them to chase up their snouts to see if they can get any information about high-end stolen goods being circulated at the moment? Or they might hear about a couple of toerags spouting off about a job they did on an elderly couple just north of Haxby."

"Of course, consider it done. And I appreciate the offer of help as well. You might regret that," Karen said with a wink as the three of them stood up and headed back to their offices.

9

KAREN GATHERED the team round the whiteboard. The room was stuffy and hot. It felt like the furnace was on full blast as a wave of heat smothered her. A combination of a lack of sleep and a long day at the office had taken its toll on Karen as tiredness crept up on her. She stifled a yawn and hid it behind her hand. After ordering in food, the desks were littered with empty cartons. Most of her officers were due to have clocked off a few hours ago, but standing there and surveying her team, she felt an immense sense of pride that most of them had stayed because they wanted a result so much.

"Right, let's crack through this. Thank you all for staying late today, I appreciate it. But once we're done catching up, I want all of you to go home, except for the late shift, of course." A few officers laughed as they ribbed the team members staying behind. "Anything to report?"

Ed waved a piece of paper in the air to catch Karen's attention. "We've reviewed the last set of call logs again and carried out phone triangulation on all three phone numbers. None of them made a call after they set off on the camping trip. Nor were any calls recorded as being answered from their parents." Ed shrugged a shoulder. "The area they were heading to is bad for a phone signal. I guess that might be the reason their parents were unable to get through to them."

Karen turned and looked at the map. The area round Kilburn was remote, wooded, with very little in the way of buildings. "Ed, what did the triangulation throw up?"

"We've identified several pings close by in Osgodby, Hambleton, and High Kilburn, which appeared to follow their route, then nothing after that. I assume they lost signal as they ventured into a wooded area. The strange thing is that all three of their phones pinged at a location twenty miles away within hours of them being reported missing. A place called Pickering, which is on the edge of the North Yorkshire Moors National Park."

Karen tapped her fingers on the map searching for the location before stabbing her finger on the word Pickering. She grabbed a black marker and circled the location. She tapped on Yearsley Woods. "This doesn't make sense. They were supposed to be camping in Kilburn. After they were reported missing, their phones pinged over twenty miles east in Pickering, and then they found Georgia's body in Yearsley Woods, which is about twenty miles back in the opposite direction towards Kilburn."

"Perhaps the killer is very familiar with that area. He may live close by?" Belinda suggested.

Karen nodded and agreed. In her mind, whoever it was knew the area well. If he had abducted all three, which was Karen's current line of thinking, it appeared as if he'd moved them all round before finally disposing of Georgia's body in Yearsley Woods. "Why Pickering? What's there?" Karen said, throwing the questions out to the team.

"Nothing of significance," Bel replied. "It's a small market town with a couple of thousand inhabitants. Quite a lot of visitors stop off in Pickering before making their way across to the national park. It also has the main route between Thirsk and Scarborough running right through it."

"Okay. Jade and I will take a drive over to Pickering tomorrow morning before heading back to the crime scene. I want to take another look at the location."

Dan shifted in his chair. "Karen, we've reviewed their social media profiles. Nothing springs out as being of interest. There were also no unusual bank transactions. No one has used their cards or gained access to their accounts against their will. We are still waiting for more feedback from local officers who are speaking to their university friends. But again, we haven't received any flags as a follow-up."

Karen blew out her cheeks and stared at the ceiling. Not only was she hot and bothered, but tired and frustrated. She needed a result fast, or Detective Superintendent Kelly was going to fry her. A few of her officers shed titbits of information, and before she could say anything else, her phone vibrated on the table next to her. She recognised the number straightaway. It was DCI Lewis from Swansea. "Okay, team, listen up. I need to take this call. Jade can wrap up with you and then after that I want you lot to piss off home." Karen grabbed her phone and headed down the corridor.

"DCI Lewis, you're a hard man to track down." Karen headed back to her office and closed the door behind her. She dropped into her chair and regretted it straight away as it wrapped round her, willing her to relax.

The DCI laughed. "I could say the same about you. Call me Owen."

"Karen," she replied.

"No, it's Owen, not Karen," he teased.

"Ha ha, very funny. It's nice to know you've got a sense of humour at this time of night. Thanks for getting back to me."

"You've got to have a sense of humour in this job, or it will kill you."

Karen shook her head. Black humour was one of the many ways to cope with the demands of the job.

He took on a serious tone. "How are you getting on with the investigation? Oh, and thanks for a copy of the post-mortem report as well. Bloody grim reading."

"Slow. Bloody slow. This is the biggest challenge I've faced since moving from London. The lack of CCTV. You can't scratch your arse in London without being caught on a dozen cameras. Here, you can literally commit murder and not be seen. We are short on forensics as well. The thread from her eyelids is being analysed at the moment, as are the small clothing fibres found on her body. We've not found foreign DNA on her. No saliva, semen, or blood... Other than her own blood, of course."

"That good, huh?"

Karen tipped her head back and closed her eyes. "Yep. That good. Have you got anything of interest from your end?" She heard Owen sigh.

"My officers have been talking to the friends and families. All three women come from solid, respectable families. No money worries, no run-ins with the authorities, their parents are all in successful careers, and Georgia, Raveena, and Louisa excelled academically."

Karen's chest sunk at the news and her shoulders sagged. Listening to Owen's feedback only made Georgia's death more tragic, and the plight of the other two more pressing. "I've got another press release going out first thing tomorrow morning. I checked the case file updates online a few hours ago, the NCA haven't been able to match up the MO to previous offenders, and there's nothing been flagged up on prisoner release records for the last twelve months for killers with a similar MO."

"Worth checking back further than twelve months?"

"Yes. I'm going to ask my team to look at the past five years. There's also the possibility that whoever committed this crime may have come into this country and so hasn't appeared on anyone's radar. We've begun enquiries overseas. It's a long shot, but I need to cover every angle."

"I agree, Karen. It's getting late and I need sleep. You're not staying late, are you?" he asked.

"No. I'm heading off too. I'll call you as soon as I have more information."

"Same here. Night, Karen."

Karen cut the call and groaned, before dragging her weary body off the chair and back into the SCU, picking up her handbag and coat on the way. Most of her team had gone home with just half a dozen officers remaining. She strolled over to the incident board and stared at the pictures of all three young women again, hoping in a warped way that one of them could communicate with her telepathically to let her know where they were.

"I promise I'll do whatever I can to find you," she whispered. "I know your parents are waiting for you and they want you home safely. We all do." With that, she threw on her coat and said good night to her team.

10

WITH A MAP in hand and a flask of coffee, Karen set off with Jade for Pickering at first light. Karen pulled rank and made Jade drive, though in reality, Karen preferred being the passenger so she could admire the landscape which had grown on her the more she adopted York as her new home.

The moors, hills, and valleys were rarely out of sight whichever direction they drove in, but as they headed north, the ruggedness of the landscape shifted and served as a reminder of how little had changed over the decades... and probably centuries. A vastness of undulating greens and browns sprinkled the valley hills, small crops of dwellings peppered the landscape, and sheep and cattle roamed freely in the fields.

As Karen's gaze relaxed into the distance, she pondered how even the hills ahead seemed to be slumbering and silent. They had a hypnotic effect on her. The landscape and vast emptiness appeared to calm her, melt away her stress, and leave her in an almost Zen-like state.

Karen smiled. At this rate, she'd be lighting incense sticks round the house, meditating, and enjoying sound baths.

"You okay?" Jade asked, catching her boss grinning to herself.

"Yes. I was thinking of how much has changed in my life since coming here. As a London girl, I never anticipated enjoying the countryside as much as I do. So much less grief than the hustle and crazy bustle of London life."

"And the constant firefight against crime."

"You're not wrong there, Jade."

Karen checked her map when she saw the first road signs for Pickering. The rugged landscape levelled out into fields, before the first signs of life appeared up ahead. From what she could see on the map and on her phone, Pickering was a small town with more than its fair share of cafés and bed and breakfasts that catered to the walking community and holidaymakers.

"The triangulation data indicated that the phones were picked up just north of the town," Karen said.

Jade followed Karen's instructions through charming residential streets of Yorkstone brick houses, with their distinctive sandy buff colour containing hints of silver and grey, unique to the region. Even with the change in seasons, the town felt busy as locals went about daily life and visitors strolled along peering into shop windows to while away time.

No sooner had they entered the town than they were already leaving its limits and heading back into the countryside to what appeared to be a residential lodge for students.

A few minutes later, Jade pulled up and checked the surroundings. "Why here?"

Karen seemed very bewildered as she stepped out of the car and rested her hands on her hips. The sign on the building stated it was a residential centre for student learning. Karen attempted to open the door, but found it locked. They walked round the perimeter, but there were no signs of life. Dense forest wrapped round it on three sides and trails snaked off between the trees. Karen called the number on the board and got through to a caretaker manager who confirmed that the centre was only open during the spring and summer months on a full-time basis, and only by appointment during the winter.

"Could the killer have a den out there somewhere?" Jade said, pointing towards the forest beyond the centre.

Karen shrugged. "I'm thinking more like he kept them captive here for a while or disposed of one of them." The thought sent a shiver through Karen as she sighed. "Jade, can you get NPAS up in the air to see if they can pick up a heat source somewhere in the forest. It's worth a try in case one of them is still being held captive out there. Can you also arrange for a cadaver dog?"

With Jade making the call, Karen walked round the treeline and looked through the trees and the dense vegetation. It would be a nightmare to search this area and may not further her investigation. But she had already made a promise to find the killer and bring Raveena and Louisa home safely.

"Done." Jade put her phone back inside her coat. "NPAS will be here in about half an hour. The K9 unit will be over about the same time."

"Okay, let's check in with them a bit later. In the meantime, let's head to the next location."

They set off again, and it wasn't long before they arrived at the second triangulation site, a small huddle of holiday cottages in a remote and picturesque spot.

"This is taking the piss." Karen stepped from the car and walked towards the nearest cottage. She told Jade to start at the other end and meet in the middle. Six out of the seven cottages were occupied. Karen could see that three of the six cottages were inhabited when she stared through the windows, but they didn't answer her knock. She imagined the occupants had already gone out for the day to explore the local landscape and made a mental note to send officers this evening to make enquiries. The holidaymakers in the remaining cottages all checked out and confirmed they had seen nothing suspicious here since their arrival a few days ago.

Frustrated and annoyed, they headed off to the final location which turned out to be a pub offering accommodation, but judging by its dilapidated state, it hadn't been occupied for some time and required refurbishment. They walked round the building to find it was securely boarded up and locked, with no signs of forced entry. Even the locks showed early signs of corrosion. The outbuildings were the same. There were no signs of discarded rubbish or recent human activity at all.

"I don't get this." Jade leant against the car bonnet as she took in the emptiness of their surroundings. "Did he bring them here as well? Maybe he was scouting these locations as potential places to keep them? Or, as you said, to dispose of their bodies?"

Karen contemplated the situation, folding her arms across her chest and chewing on her bottom lip. "You could be right on both counts, but I'm also considering the possibility that he did this intentionally. What if he drove round these locations to confuse us? He knew we would check their phones and GPS tracking. My guess is he went on a long drive with or without the women and had their phones on so it would appear like they were at these locations, when all along, they weren't. It was all part of his plan to throw us off the scent and confuse us."

Jade nodded. "If he did, he's a clever shit."

"Contact NPAS and the K9 unit. Give them the location of the cottages and pub. We need a sweep of these areas too. If they pick up anything, we can get the search teams involved."

Karen walked round the deserted car park of the pub. Moors surrounded the whole area. A very bleak and barren place with gorse, overgrown wild grass, and dense woodland. The perfect place to hide or bury a body. Needle in a haystack sprung to mind. She was interrupted in her thoughts when her phone vibrated in her back pocket. Pulling it out, she saw Belinda's number on her screen.

"Bel, everything okay?"

"Karen... W..." Silence. "Can... me?" Silence. "Bad..."

"Fuck sake. Shitty phone signal, Bel." Karen pulled the phone away from her ear to see there was only one bar of signal. She moved round the car park to find a better reception and tried again when two bars popped up on her screen. Karen redialled. "Sorry, Bel, the signal is terrible out here. Can you hear me okay, now?"

"Yes, better. It's patchy from my end. Where are you?"

"In the arse end of nowhere. Or more commonly known as the former pub and B & B, The Blacksmiths, in Pickering. Now permanently closed. Been on a wild goose chase today. I'll tell you about it when we see you."

"Okay, well I've got an update for you. The team has been called to a discovery. We think we've found where the women were camping. I'll send you over the details and see you there."

"Great. See you soon." Karen hung up. "Jade! We've got to go," Karen shouted as she hurried back to the car.

11

Twenty-five minutes later, they arrived in Kilburn. Jade had covered the distance at speed as Karen had encouraged her to go faster.

They changed into their wellies before making their way from the grass verge to where Belinda waited for them.

"What do we have, Bel?" Karen asked. Her eyes darted between Belinda and the taped off area about a hundred yards into the forest.

"Search team officers came across a recent campsite with personal belongings connected to Louisa. The forest ranger is on his way to meet us."

"Okay, let's take a look." Karen headed off towards the taped off area with Belinda and Jade in tow. "What personal possessions?"

"A black rainproof jacket with Louisa's name printed on the inside pocket, along with a personalised scarf carrying her name, and a pair of pink muddy Nike trainers."

"The size of the trainers?"

"Five."

Karen trudged through the long grass, her wellies squelching in the sodden soil. "Unless we are dealing with a small male who likes pink trainers, it's likely they belong to one of the three women."

Up ahead, Karen saw the first signs of heightened police activity as officers walked in a line searching in the undergrowth, long sticks being used to move piles of leaves and vegetation in search of evidence. Karen and her team dipped under the tape and stepped on to the metal foot plates put down by SOCO to create a safe path through to the campsite.

When they reached it, the three of them stood in silence to get a first impression. A small pile of sticks formed a makeshift fire. But there was little evidence of charring which indicated that starting a fire might not have been possible due to the damp conditions and the storm. Despite the shelter provided by a large canopy of branches, the combination of strong winds and driving rain would have made it almost impossible to start with the small pile of sticks.

A small sheet of tarpaulin lay close by, with long sticks tied to each corner. Karen thought it may have been used to cover their makeshift fire from the rain. Three self-inflating camping mats and sleeping bags lay tossed to one side among the debris of broken branches and mounds of leaves.

Jade's eyes scanned the immediate area. "No rucksacks or utensils?"

Belinda nodded. "Perhaps the killer forced them to take their rucksacks? Less evidence for us?"

Karen stared off into the distance as she thought this through. Belinda's suggestion was plausible. Alternatively, he could have just abducted them and returned later to remove their belongings, which would explain why their phones were picked up from three different locations. Maybe he was looking for places where he could dump their belongings.

"Maybe," Karen replied. "Did he also come back and take Raveena's car? We've not found it."

Jade scratched her forehead. "What if they had to abandon their camp because of the storm? They then headed back to Raveena's car, but they broke down somewhere and that's where the killer picked them up. You'd be nuts to stay out in a storm. I know they're used to it and have probably dealt with treacherous conditions on previous camping expeditions, but this one was pretty bad." Jade circled her hand in an arc round them. "Look at the amount of fallen debris from the trees round us. Not just leaves, but big broken branches. You'd know about it if one of those hit you on the head. Perhaps they deemed it too dangerous and called off the trip, but didn't have enough time to roll up their sleeping bags and mattresses, so they just made a dash for the car?"

"Your guess is as good as mine. There are lots of potential outcomes. We don't know whether the killer intercepted them here, or somewhere out there." Karen pointed back towards the road. "It's hard to tell if there are any signs of a struggle here because the place is such a mess. And it will be difficult to pick up traces of human blood because most of it would have washed away." Karen studied the crime scene investigators kneeling on rubber mats as they meticulously examined the ground round them.

"They chose the location well," Belinda said. "Without the storm, the conifers would offer them decent protection, and there's a stream about ten minutes in that direction." Belinda pointed to her left. "They could wash their cutlery and canteen sets. Raveena's car would be a short walk away because my guess is she would have parked where we did."

"Yes, and it also means it would have been easy for our killer to have found them," Karen added.

Belinda blew out a breath. "There is a possibility that the killer turned up here. The girls panicked and made a dash for Raveena's car. Georgia was too slow and was captured. Raveena and Louisa tried to get away and crashed, and the killer found them and took them as well."

Guesses. That's all they had with no hard evidence or tangible leads. As Karen stood there, it felt like the blind leading the blind.

"We need to double our efforts with the local units to find the car. I'll speak to the Super to see if we can pull in more resources," Karen said. "We should consider the possibility that it is lying abandoned in a ditch."

"Well, let's hope it's just the car and not Raveena and Louisa as well," Jade added, before they headed back to the car to meet with the forest ranger.

12

KAREN NOTICED a slight shift in the weather as she appeared from the forest and marched across tall, wet grass. The air was thick and swollen with moisture, the sky low, and grey, and a fine drizzle fell from the broody clouds. It wasn't a downpour as such, but a fine mist that seemed to soak you to the skin in a matter of minutes.

Jade fumed as she picked up the pace. "My bloody hair."

Karen flipped up the hood from her jacket and stuffed her hands in her pockets. Head down, she quickened her steps to catch up with Jade. Belinda didn't seem bothered. A local lass, she was hardier than them. Northerners always took the piss out of southerners for not coping too well with inclement weather, and though in the past she would have defended southerners until her last breath, she held respect for those up north who seemed unfazed by the harsh winter months.

"That's the ranger," Belinda offered as she walked alongside Karen.

Karen looked up and saw a man step from a green

Land Rover and make his way towards them, rubbing his hands to keep warm.

He extended his hand. "Tim Price, forest ranger."

"DCI Karen Heath, York police." Karen shook his hand. She noticed the calluses on his palms and the dry roughness of his skin. With his ruddy, weathered face and salt and pepper beard, he looked like a man who'd spent most of his life working outdoors. He wore green combats, a cream T-shirt, a green hoodie, and a black baseball cap. Karen estimated him to be in his late forties or early fifties.

Price nodded his head in acknowledgement. "I saw your press appeals. They been helpful?"

Karen shook her head. "Not yet. It's still early days in the investigation, but we have two missing people at the moment, and one in the morgue."

Price rubbed his chubby fingers through his beard. "Very sad news. It's not something you'd expect round here. Last time we had a body in those Yearsley Woods was over ten years ago. Rough sleeper. They found his remains three months later. With the amount of wildlife we have in those woods, you can imagine that there wasn't much left of him."

"We've found their campsite. Our forensic team is undertaking a detailed examination and we've got officers combing the immediate area for any evidence linked to the three women."

Price nodded again and stared over Karen's shoulder towards a hive of activity in the forest. "It's a very secluded area. Some people like to camp here because of its remoteness. They like to feel cut off from civilisation for a few days. Nigh on impossible to get a phone signal in there."

"As we've found out," Karen said in agreement.

"Phone providers have been looking to install extra masts in the area, but there's been a lot of objections from the locals. They want to keep this area as natural as possible, but that doesn't really fit in with modern-day society now, does it?" Tim carried on, not waiting for a response. "The distance and direction of the nearest mobile tower can have a huge effect on the quality of your phone calls. Add to that the transmission power of the tower itself, which is often greater than the transmission power of your phone, which means you could have five bars on your screen and yet be unable to hold a conversation."

"Are you saying that they could have had full strength on their phones, but their phones weren't powerful enough to make a call?" Karen asked for clarity.

"Yes. And the local terrain isn't particularly conducive for mobile networks. The hills, the atmospheric conditions, cloud cover, and dense trees can all affect the phone signal." Price nodded over Karen's shoulder towards the woods. "Radio signals will bounce off obstacles, creating a multipath, thus decreasing mobile coverage."

Tim zipped up his hoodie to shield him from the worst of the rain, which had changed direction and now slapped him in the face, the rain droplets clinging to his beard. "Thinking back to the night they went missing; we had a terrific storm sitting over us with a couple of flashes of lightning and a few claps of thunder. That's enough to scrub any phone reception, even in the middle of town."

"Okay, that's helpful. I think we are at a disadvantage because of that, but stating the obvious, there is a visible lack of CCTV in the area."

Price laughed as his shoulders shook.

"We are also short of witnesses, too. It feels like we're running round this investigation with a great big bloody blindfold on," Karen said, her voice tinged with frustration.

"Have you spoken to Charles Knight?"

Karen furrowed her brow. "Who's he?"

"The Yearsley hermit. He's lived in the Yearsley Woods for fifteen years now. Ran away when he was eighteen years old after being abused by his father. His parents were incredibly wealthy. Millionaires. His father owned an import and export business." Price nodded in reflection. "But Charles turned his back on their wealth and on his inheritance and disappeared. He turned up in the woods not long after and has lived there ever since."

"You talk about his parents in the past tense?" Jade chipped in.

"That's right. Parents died in a boating accident in Sardinia ten years ago."

"And their estate?" Jade asked.

"Believe it or not, they left everything to charity. Surprisingly, they didn't include any other living relatives as part of the inheritance. It created a huge kerfuffle. Courts, solicitors, legal teams. The whole works. But the will was very clear, business, the properties, the money, all signed over to a charity."

"Shit," Jade said, raising a brow.

"Indeed. Might be worth having a chat with Charles. It's as if these woods are his back garden, he roams them so freely. Although he moves about a bit, this tends to be his base. Charles has a camp deep inside the woods. If you head thirty minutes in that direction," Price said, jabbing a finger towards the east, "you'll come across it."

"Does Charles have any contact with anyone these days?" Karen asked.

Price shrugged. "Not much. There are a few residents who come every so often with boxes of provisions. A retired doctor stops by and checks on his health. The people around here really like him. He wouldn't harm a fly. Don't annoy him and he won't annoy you. He wants to be left alone."

"Okay, Tim. Thanks for your time." Karen extended her hand.

"Any time." Tim shook her hand and turned back towards his Land Rover.

———

FORTY MINUTES LATER, Karen, Jade, and Belinda stumbled across a well-established campsite in Yearsley Woods. To one side was a hut, constructed from sheets of plywood and painted with a sticky black substance which Karen assumed was tar. A couple of corrugated sheets of metal formed its roof. A spit sat above a circle of stones with the remnants of charred wood from a fire.

"Welcome to my crib. Let me show you what I've done with the place," Bel said in a fake gruff American accent, mimicking the MTV show where American celebrities showed the TV crew round their palatial residences. The joke went over Karen's head, causing her to narrow her eyes in confusion.

Jade laughed. "You not down with the hood?"

"Will you both shut up! You're making me out to be a dinosaur. I've heard of MTV."

The three of them split up and wandered round the campsite. "Hello!" Karen shouted. "It's the police. Is anyone here?"

A wall of silence greeted the question. Karen was certain this wasn't an abandoned site. A few T-shirts and jogging bottoms hung from an improvised clothes rail strung up between two trees. A stash of tin cans of food laid neatly stacked in a plastic tub beside the hut. More alarmingly, a few machetes hung from hooks screwed into a tree.

"No one here," Belinda said, meeting up with the others.

"If you're out there watching us, you're not in any trouble. We only want to ask you a few questions. You might be able to help us." Karen's loud voice echoed through the trees. They stood in silence for a few seconds listening out for any signs of movement. Nothing.

"Maybe he's out foraging or something. The light is fading. I think we'd be better off coming back again tomorrow." Karen pulled up the collar on her coat and zipped it up to shield her from the creeping chill.

Jade agreed enthusiastically as she nodded. "Sounds good to me. I left my hand sanitiser in the car. God knows what I've picked up from touching *things* round here."

"You and your bloody OCD." Karen tutted in amusement as she turned and headed back towards the car.

13

I CAN'T STOP the shivering. Even though I'm dressed, my bones are rattling. My teeth are chattering. Why? Why are we here?

I know Georgia is dead. I heard the ear-shattering screams. Though I clamped my eyes shut and held my hands over my ears, the sounds seeped in, drilling into my brain like a high-speed drill. No matter how hard I tried to drown out the relentless wave of harrowing shrills that tore from her throat, nothing provided relief. In her final moments, as her throat gurgled and spluttered, I heard her crying and felt the gut-wrenching pain right along with my friend. Whatever he did to her, it sounded terrifying. I never imagined I would hear sounds like that from another human being.

I'm so cold. I want this nightmare to end. The corner I sit in doesn't seem far enough away. It doesn't offer me the shelter I need. My clothes are damp from where I couldn't control myself. I was scared to move to use the bucket. Fear paralysed my body.

The lights only come on for a few hours a day. The rest

of the time I'm sitting in darkness. I know he's watching me. There's a red light blinking on a camera which hangs from the ceiling.

My fingers are raw and bleeding from scratching the walls. My stomach aches, but it's not from hunger, it's from where he kicked me when I was lying on the floor. He just kept kicking me until I stopped making any sounds. I've learnt the hard way. If you make too much noise, it annoys him, and the beatings are a punishment.

I can hear Louisa sobbing in the room next to me. "Louisa," I whisper, keeping my voice as low as possible. He can hear our every word, our cries, and our sobs. But I need to speak to Louisa.

"Louisa, can you hear me?"

The whimpers from Louisa's cell die down. I'm struggling to keep it together, but I know she's lost it. She has hysterical fits and screams at the top of her voice. She bangs on the door and pleads for help. But that only attracts more attention. She's had it a lot worse than me.

I place my head against the wall. "Louisa, we're going to be okay. Someone is going to find us. They know we are missing. It's just a matter of time."

Can she hear me?

"You need to hang on in there. We can get out of here, I promise. Maybe we need to distract him or pretend one of us isn't well." My whispers echo off the cold concrete and slap me in the face. Whether or not she's heard me, I'm unsure, but I need her to know that she's not alone.

Time isn't on our side. Georgia wasn't here for long. And now I am left wondering who will be next? Perhaps it's me as I hear the jingling of keys.

14

When will these women realise the concept of compliance? He shook his head in annoyance as he watched them on the laptop only yards away. If she thought he had heard nothing, she was sorely wrong.

The Asian one had a bit of fire in her, a defiant streak that still needed sorting. He stared at the other one, Louisa. She'd lost the plot. He'd noticed chunks of hair on the floor the last time he'd checked on her. She'd been banging her head against the walls and tugging at her damp, matted brown hair. The man wondered how much longer she'd survive. Yet, she was a fantastic source of amusement, and his viewers preferred her to stay the longest. The cruel bastards wanted to see her suffer. A smirk spread across his face.

Let's see what reaction this sparks, he thought as he rose and headed to Raveena's cell.

The man unlocked the door, his hulking colossal frame filling the doorway. The light behind him filled the darkened room. Raveena shielded her eyes as she pressed her body deep into the corner of the room, pulling her knees up to her chest.

"Please don't hurt me," she begged in a shaky, croaky voice.

"You know what happens when you break the rules," he growled. "I don't know how many times I need to tell you this, but the more you annoy me, the more your body is going to hurt."

Tears tumbled down Raveena's face as she snuffled. "I... I... Promise... Not to say anything else," she pleaded.

"That bollocks isn't going to wash with me any more." He marched into the room and grabbed her by the hair, dragging her weak body across the floor. Raveena tried to keep up with him and scurried across the floor on her hands and knees. He raised his fist and brought it down across the side of her face. A scream tore from her throat as she threw her hands up in defence.

"I'm... Please. I'm sorry!" Raveena sobbed.

"What have I told you about screaming? I want silence. You have a choice. I either kick the shit out of you or I go next door and hurt your friend so much that you'll wonder what I've done to her."

The man leant down and grabbed Raveena by the hair, again yanking her head back so that her face was in full view of the camera which hung from the ceiling.

"Shall I?" he shouted, staring at the camera. "What's it worth to you?"

He waited a few seconds before he punched her again. The cracking of a bone echoed round the room.

He pushed her back down on to the floor and watched as she curled up into a small embryonic ball. Her body trembled as she groaned in pain. A grin spread across his face as he pulled a pair of pliers from his back pocket and knelt down beside her. One of his large hands grabbed her face and squeezed her cheeks until her mouth opened.

Spittle and blood spewed from Raveena's mouth as he thrust his pliers between her lips and clamped the jaws round the first tooth he could reach. He pulled the pliers from left to right, the petite woman's face moving in time with his efforts. She squirmed on the floor, her squeals and cries spurring him on as he gritted his teeth and pulled harder. The crunch of flesh rippled through the pliers and into his fingers as a tooth finally loosened. With a final yank, he pulled it from her mouth and held it up towards the camera. A satisfied grin spread across his face before he tossed it to one side.

He stood up and left the room for a moment, leaving the door open behind him. He didn't worry about her making a break for it because she was too broken and in pain. Besides, he would only be gone for a few seconds. He went over to the laptop and checked the feed. Comments streamed in. "Yes, one more." "Give it to the bitch." "Just one tooth?" "I'll pay good money for her dirty knickers."

The man grinned. "Sick bastards," he said with a maniacal laugh. It seemed the more he hurt them, the more the audience got worked up. He left his laptop, the comments still streaming in, as he returned and checked on Raveena once more. She hadn't moved and in the shady light he saw blood oozing from her mouth. He turned and locked the door behind him.

They loved it, he thought as he returned to the screen. The votes for Raveena shot up higher than he expected. Whether it was a temporary spike or his audience wanting her as his next victim, he was unsure.

He pulled up a chair and interacted with his audience. The requests continued to pour in. "Cut off her finger."

"Use a knife to play noughts and crosses on her belly."
"Shove a broom handle up her." "Plunge a screwdriver
into her ear canal." His eyes widened in shock and
surprise at the brutality of some requests. Never in his
wildest dreams did he imagine he could earn money from
people round the globe for torturing women in this way.

He checked his IP connections. They were all hidden,
with his connections to the internet being bounced all
round the globe using a roaming VPN, a virtual private
network. Many years of being in this game had taught him
how to use the Dark Web to stay under the radar of the
authorities. He would hide his IP address, which is an
internet address linked to a property, and if anyone tried
to find him, the address could appear in Guatemala one
day, Mexico the next, then France, Spain, America, and
Australia. It was impossible to trace his location. But he
needed to be careful. He had learnt from speaking to
many virtual contacts across the globe that it was important to switch to a new VPN every few days to dilute his
digital breadcrumb trail further.

There was much for him to do, so he minimised the
screen and left his audience to chat with each other while
the voting continued. In the meantime, he opened up his
network settings and began hooking up to a new VPN. *It
will be tight*, he thought as he checked his watch, with half
an hour before he needed to head off to work, and still so
much to accomplish.

15

Cold and damp, Karen and her team returned to the office. The chill outdoors seeped into her bones, leaving her stiff and lethargic as she plopped down in her chair and welcomed the heat from the radiators on her hands for a few moments.

She wanted to close her eyes and sleep, but sleep was a luxury for everyone in the unit. Many of her team had been working over the hours they needed to, and only the ones with families were sticking to regular shift patterns. With budget constraints across the county, the force had been unable to afford paid overtime as they had suffered cuts to personnel, equipment, and overtime budgets. She had witnessed it first-hand in London, where the Met expansion programme for the refurbishment of many stations had been cancelled across several boroughs. Budget cuts also extended to closing down many front desk services that were a staple in every police station up and down the country.

Karen logged into her computer and checked the case file for the updates from her team. The latest press release had garnered a lot of feedback, and though she knew that most of it would be irrelevant and unhelpful, the team needed to sift through every call and email from the public. Sightings of the missing women were thin on the ground. A few members of the public thought they'd spotted groups of women traipsing across the hills laden with rucksacks. But as she looked into each enquiry further, it was clear that no one had spotted the group of three women close-up, but merely from a distance. It wasn't the news Karen needed, and with nothing to go on at the moment, the last person she wanted to bump into would be her boss, Detective Superintendent Laura Kelly.

The extra resources Jade organised this morning were scanning all three locations. NPAS swept all three sites and found multiple heat sources, as well as movement along trails and across the hills, and from their position in the helicopter, it was easy to identify and eliminate most of the people they saw. The ground teams received anything suspicious and moved to each location to verify any potential sightings.

Despite the unlikelihood of finding anything, she had no choice but to utilise all the resources she had to cover the vast area. Officers were already deployed to visit the cottages later to catch up with holidaymakers that Karen hadn't been able to speak to this morning.

The more she thought about this, the more she believed the killer had driven round all three locations searching for a suitable site before giving up and moving on. There was a slim possibility that the killer had already imprisoned his victims somewhere, and he was determined to lay down false tracks to slow down the police investigation.

Karen's phone disturbed her thoughts. It was DCI

Owen Lewis from Swansea. She took a deep breath and answered. "Owen, how are things with you?"

"Hi, Karen, I was about to ask you the same thing."

"I beat you to it. Anything useful in the background searches of our three women that might be of help to us?"

Karen listened to the shuffling of papers at the other end.

"Possibly," Owen replied. "We have interviewed their friends and family in the Swansea area. Our visits included the gyms they were members of, the charity work they engaged in, and the places where they worked part-time. We are doing everything we can to be thorough."

Karen sensed the tension in his voice, his deep breaths alluding to the frustration he felt.

"So what did you find?"

"This might interest you. Georgia had a boyfriend. Karim Ahmed. A bit of a wrong one. She split up with him before university. He didn't take kindly to her calling it off."

"Go on," Karen prompted.

"Karim is known to us. He is an aggressive individual and into supplying drugs. He hangs round with associates on the Heol Gwyrosydd estate in Penlan, Swansea."

"I wouldn't expect someone like Georgia with her background and the fact she's at university, to hang round with a dealer?"

"I agree. And so did her parents. We spoke to them, and they mentioned how much they hated her being with him. It led to a lot of family arguments between them. Georgia was quite stubborn and in love with him. Karim showered her with gifts, and always seemed at odds with Georgia's parents every time he came round."

"He sounds like a lovely, charming man." Karen sighed.

"Hardly boyfriend or husband material," Owen added. "Here's the crunch. When they split up, he continued to follow her round the city. He said he would follow her to university, and he did frequently. Georgia told him to back off or she would call the police. And for a while, he seemed to heed the warning, until he appeared wherever she was."

This was progress as far as Karen was concerned. She felt saddened for Georgia, but everything she had heard from Owen suggested this was worth following up. "Can you bring him in for questioning?"

"We would if we could. We need to find out where the slippery sod is."

"Agreed. Question him about his last known movements and when he last saw Georgia. Get a ping on his phone data for the last week."

"It might take a bit of time to find him. He moves about in the shadows, and he hasn't got a permanent address. He tends to sofa-surf."

Karen scrunched her face. Everything she heard about Karim suggested he was the complete opposite to Georgia, so why was she interested in him to begin with? Had he supplied drugs to Georgia?

"Well, see what you can do, Owen. We need to get results quick."

"We'll do our best. The case has affected the citizens of Swansea. Three women in their prime being abducted and one being murdered has rattled the city. I've lost count of the number of vigils taking place. I'm getting a lot of heat at my end now as well."

"Join the club. This is a multi-force investigation now. My team spoke to Leeds police and the other forces involved, and they couldn't turn up anything at their end. They spoke to university friends and lecturers, and no one had a bad word to say about any of the women. Not once did any of them suggest they were in danger or concerned about someone stalking or threatening them."

"You do realise we're probably dealing with a stranger attack."

"It looks that way, and that worries me. Anyway, I need to head back out, so I'll touch base with you soon."

"Okay, Karen. Speak soon."

Karen cut the call and placed her phone on the desk as she tipped her head back in the chair. The investigation was going nowhere, and it was slowly grinding to a halt. Thoughts crept into her mind whether Raveena and Louisa were still alive. She hoped so. One body was bad enough, but to be the SIO with three bodies was something that every officer up and down the country would talk about for a long time.

She rose from her chair and rotated her shoulders to relieve the tension. A burning spot of pain burrowed deep in between her shoulders. "Right, let's get this shit done," Karen muttered as she grabbed her phone and damp coat, picking up Belinda and Dan on her way out.

16

A**N** **INKY** **BLACK** canvas surrounded them as Karen pulled up on the grassy verge close to Yearsley Woods. Thankfully, her headlights illuminated the road ahead of them, two white beacons of light like long fingers, offering familiarity to the area. Yet, as soon as she shut off the engine, it appeared that the surroundings were closing around them. As she stepped from the car, Karen noticed the distinct drop in temperature. A cloying moistness hung in the air smothering them.

"It doesn't get much darker than this." Dan came round to the rear of the car and popped the boot open before changing out of his shoes and into his black wellington boots. Karen and Bel did the same before they headed off.

Thankfully, all three of them had standard-issue torches with them, which helped them to navigate their way through the wet grassland.

A chilling silence surrounded them, only broken by the sounds of their wellies squelching in the muddy soil beneath their feet. Their torches formed an arc of light, which picked out the uneven ground ahead of them as they reached the treeline. The woods were a dark, quiet, and mysterious place at night. Karen sensed icy chills lightly caressing her back as if the tentacles of winter were slowly creeping into her clothes.

Light from the torches bounced off the thick trunks and bushes that surrounded them. A bed of leaves cushioned their feet as they trod across the wet and slippery ground. From her experience of walking round Epping Forest while she lived in Epping, she knew the forest floor was often thick with underbrush, exposed twisty and gnarly tree roots, and fallen leaves, which made it hard to move round, especially in the winter months.

It was an eerie place, with only the sounds of their breath as Belinda and Dan walked alongside her.

"Shit," Belinda shouted as she tripped over a hidden tree root.

"Are you okay?" Dan asked, turning his light towards her.

"Yeah, stubbed my bloody toe."

Their journey towards the hermit's den appeared to take twice as long as when they had last visited. Maybe because it was harder to get their bearings through the woods at night. There were no reference points, no signs, and nothing but trees... bloody trees.

"Can you smell that?" Karen paused. All three sniffed the air.

"A fire? Burning wood?" Belinda suggested.

"Smells like it," Karen replied. "It's coming from that direction," she added, checking the compass app on her phone and pointed north-east.

It was a further ten minutes before Karen spotted the first signs of the camp. Small yellow and orange flames danced and pirouetted in between the trees. "Right, watch your step and stay vigilant. These are his woods, not ours. He knows this area like the back of his hand."

"He might be watching us now," Belinda whispered, her voice laced with concern. She scanned the shadowy surroundings. "Shit, he could've been trailing us for all this time, and we wouldn't know."

They continued to walk in silence, slowing their pace even further, each one of them alert for any signs of movement or danger. Dan carried his retractable baton in his hand. Belinda had hers clipped to her waist, and Karen had hers in the pocket of her coat, her fingers curled round the handle in readiness. There were no signs as Karen reached the small clearing and felt the warm orange glow from a fire in the middle bathe her face.

"I can imagine a circle of pagan worshippers doing a ritual round this fire," Karen said.

Belinda stopped by a metal plate on the floor with what looked like the remnants of a rabbit carcass. "Gross," she whispered.

"He's close." Karen joined her and slid her hand beneath the plate. "There's heat coming through the metal. Hello!" Karen shouted. Nothing. Not even the rustle of leaves or the snap of a twig. "Hello! It's the police. I know you're out there. You're not in any danger or trouble. We just need to talk to you."

"Why won't he come out?" Belinda asked.

"Maybe he's scared... or guilty," Dan chipped in.

All three of them jumped seconds later when a scream tore through the woods.

"Jesus, what was that?" Belinda squealed as she spun round in a full circle, the light from her torch bouncing off every tree trunk round them.

Dan stiffened into a defensive stance, his hands

hanging loosely by his side, his baton in one hand, ready to strike.

"Sounded like a fox to me. I used to hear them all the time in Epping," Karen said to reassure her officers.

"Please!" Karen shouted. "We need to talk to you. Tim Price, the forest ranger, suggested we speak with you. You might be able to help with our investigation following the discovery of a female body in the woods. I'm hoping you might have seen or heard something." She had a gut feeling he was lurking deep within the trees, watching their every movement. His body camouflaged in the darkness behind the hulking tree trunks and dense undergrowth even though her torch didn't pick up anything.

"This place gives me the chills. Do you know there were ancient tales of witches being killed in the woods by the locals?" Belinda's voice tremored.

"Right, okay. And you believe that, do you?" Karen replied.

Belinda shook her head. "Well, the locals believe it. Apparently, every time a witch was uncovered, they brought them here, hung them up by their ankles, and gutted them. Old folklore says that their ghosts still roam here, their spirits not released to the afterlife."

"Well, maybe the ghosts or whatever could be valuable witnesses in our investigation?" Karen said, staring at Belinda.

Dan laughed as he shook his head and turned his torch in the darkness round them. Inch by inch, he moved the beam in a full circle looking for any shadowy figure moving in between the trees.

Karen felt relieved having Dan with her. His large and muscular frame would prove useful if the hermit turned on them. An idea sprung to mind as Karen headed over to a pile of belongings by the hut. She opened a few bags and rifled through them and lifted the lids from a few boxes, rattling the pots and pans inside them. It was a long shot, but she hoped it would be enough to force him out into the open if he was protective over his belongings. Disappointment twisted Karen's features into a scowl when nothing happened.

"What do you reckon?" Dan asked. "Even if he is watching us, I doubt he's going to come out and show himself. He shies away from meeting people who come in search of him. The locals who leave boxes of food and provisions have rarely seen him, but when they come back to check, the boxes are all gone."

Karen tutted. "I fucked up. I should've called in a K9 unit. A dog would've picked up his scent and we wouldn't be standing her like numpties."

"More like scared him off and that wouldn't have done us any favours," Dan replied.

Dan had a point. "Right, let's knock it on the head for tonight. We'll try again tomorrow. I don't know about you, but I'm bloody shattered and need my bed."

Belinda didn't need to be told twice as she turned on her heels and marched off. "The sooner we get out of here, the better," she said over her shoulder as Dan and Karen followed.

17

_____

KAREN SAT at the dining table the next morning nursing a coffee while she logged online through her laptop. Her thoughts turned to her visit to Yearsley Woods last night. Not finding the hermit left her frustrated, but as she thought about it more, her attitude towards him softened. She took a sip from her mug as she flicked through emails sitting in her inbox.

The conversation about Charles's upbringing with Tim Price, the forest ranger, piqued her interest. Charles must have suffered a lot for him to walk away from his privileged life for a simple one in the woods. She wondered what was going through the young man's mind when he'd made that decision. So many young people of his age would've been enjoying a busy social life with few worries. Perhaps it wasn't just the abuse, but the expectation placed upon his young shoulders as the heir apparent that had contributed to his decision to walk away from it all and shun human contact. Was that the reason he hadn't come out from the shadows last night? Or was it unease because he now feared human interaction?

There was another theory floating round Karen's mind. Maybe he did witness something? A search of his belongings hadn't revealed any incriminating evidence linking him to the abduction and murder of Georgia and the whereabouts of Raveena and Louisa. Was he even capable of such a crime? Highly unlikely... unless he felt threatened?

Karen's mind was in disarray. She hated not being in control of an investigation. Each case in York had forced her to challenge her well-established and trusted policing methods, and it was something she was still adapting to.

She took another sip of her coffee and clicked open the email from Bart Lynch, the CSI manager. He'd prepared the forensic report for Georgia. Karen scrolled through the early explanations in search of the juicy stuff. Soil samples taken from Georgia's body matched the soil in Yearsley Woods. There were no other foreign soil particles on her body.

Something else caught her interest. Izzy had found pollen particles on the skin scrapings taken during the PM, but forensics couldn't provide further information as they needed to carry out specialist palynology analysis. That was new to Karen. She hadn't come across that term but carried on reading Bart's description.

In simple terms, he explained it was the detailed study of pollen, plant spores, fungal spores, and the microscopic remains of plants and animals. Karen raised a brow. *Interesting.* Bart added that plant and fungal spores, and pollen grains, were tiny in diameter and impossible to see with the naked eye. He believed the evidence once analysed may reveal flora or fauna that was only found in specific locations. Karen sat back in her chair as she considered his report. If that was the case, it would give her a lead on where to focus the investigation geographically. This was good news. *Well done, Bart,* she thought.

Karen continued to skim through the rest of the report. Something else drew her attention. The investigators identified the blue clothing fibres found on Georgia's skin as silk. How did silk threads get on her? Karen wondered if Georgia was wearing silk clothing before being stripped naked, or did someone wrap her body in a silk garment or sheet before dumping her?

Though the evidence was interesting and helpful, it still didn't help Karen. The investigation had also identified traces of oil and grease deposits which were industrial in nature, suggesting a link to heavy industrial or plant equipment. There were dozens of farm buildings and industrial units in the area, both in current use and disused. She didn't have the time or resources to search every single building.

"Are you going in late?" Zac walked into the kitchen doing up his tie. He came over and kissed Karen on the cheek.

"No. I thought I'd catch up on my emails to get ahead of myself before I went in for my briefing with the team."

"Any recent developments?" Zac picked up Karen's mug and took a swig from her coffee.

"Oi, get your own."

"I thought we shared everything now?" Zac teased.

"There's sharing and there's sharing. Don't tell me you can't make your own coffee. Next you'll be telling me you can't wipe your own arse."

Zac playfully rested his hands on his hips. "Why do you always have to lower the tone of the conversation? There are plenty of dodgy sites if that's your kink?"

Karen shrugged a shoulder. "It comes with years of practice. You should try doing a stint in the Met. The conversations in the station are far worse than the ones we experience on the streets."

"I don't doubt that."

Karen shut the lid on her laptop and stood, wrapping her arms round Zac's waist. "I guess I should get to the office now, unless I can persuade you to enjoy my kinks..." Karen nuzzled up to Zac and kissed his neck.

"Now you get frisky. Talk about bad timing. You'll have to put out that fire on your own. I'm due in court in thirty minutes."

Karen pulled a face. "Spoilsport. See you this evening for dinner?"

"I hope so. Court should finish by four. I know we have busy lives, but I can't wait to get home and see you... You always bring a smile to my face. Most days."

Karen frowned and playfully punched him in the chest. "You cheeky git."

Karen stuffed her laptop in her bag and kissed Zac on the lips before grabbing her coat and car keys on the way out.

18

AFTER DROPPING her bag and coat in her office, a buzz of energy greeted Karen as she walked into the SCU. A few officers were on their phones, while others were in the middle of conversations, and even though they had so little to go on, it felt like the team was determined to push on in their search for the two missing women. She grabbed a chocolate Bourbon from the packet on Preet's desk as she made her way to the front. "Don't mind if I do." She gave Preet a wink.

"Right, I checked the system first thing. We might have more information or sightings of the three women?"

Ned raised his hand. "Yes, we recovered CCTV footage from a petrol station about five miles from Yearsley Woods showing Raveena's car with all three women. Raveena stopped for petrol, and Georgia and Louisa stepped out to stretch their legs."

Karen went round to the monitor and fired up the laptop attached to it. Ned joined her and located the file before he clicked the play icon. Karen folded her arms across her chest and studied the screen. Two cameras on the forecourt picked up Raveena's black Astra as it pulled alongside a pump. Raveena stepped out and closed the door before saying something to Louisa. They must've shared a joke, because Raveena laughed before she turned and pulled the nozzle from the pump and added fuel to her car. Once finished, Raveena casually walked into the station, taking out her phone from her back pocket and fiddling with something on the screen.

"Her banking records confirmed she paid by Google Pay." Ned slid a chair closer and planted himself in it.

Georgia and Louisa looked relaxed as they chatted. Louisa pulled her hair into a ponytail and used the scrunchy from her wrist to secure her hair in place. All the while, cars passed by along the road, none of them slowing or pulling in. Karen clenched her jaw. The forecourt feed was clear, but the road beyond it was out of focus. Getting registration details would be hard.

A few minutes later, Raveena strolled out and back to her car, throwing bags of crisps at the other two. It set off another round of laughter between them. It pained Karen. They looked so happy and carefree, and she imagined the excitement they'd felt about their trip. And yet, over twenty-four hours later, they were missing, and one lay brutally murdered. Her chest tightened at the thought.

Seconds later, Raveena drove away. As Karen studied the footage, she noticed that the women showed no signs of alarm or concern. And at the time they were there, no other cars were on the forecourt.

Karen turned to Ned. "Good stuff. Can you do me a favour?"

"Sure."

"Track through the footage for thirty minutes before and after they were here and extend the time frame by another thirty minutes incrementally each way. See if anyone followed or was ahead of them. Is there any other footage which covers the road outside of the petrol station?"

"There is, but it only catches one lane, not both."

"That's a shame. But if we identify any registration plates, we could trace the owners and find out if they have dashcam footage. Ask Preet to help as we need this as soon as."

Ned nodded and returned to his desk. Karen stared at a freeze-frame of the petrol station. Someone must have seen them after this point. Karen returned to Preet's desk and nicked another Bourbon. Preet did a double take, shocked at Karen's audacity. "Sorry, I'm bloody famished today. I've only had a coffee and need sugar."

"How about I buy you a packet the next time I get myself some?" Preet teased.

"Bless you, you're all heart despite what everyone else says about you," Karen fired back.

Preet smirked as Karen moved away.

"Claire, can you do me a favour? Check the maps again and look for any buildings or dwellings on the road where this petrol station is." Karen threw a thumb over her shoulder. "I want to see if there's other CCTV or Ring footage in the direction they were travelling."

"I'll double-check. Shall I make a list and head out?"

"Yes, if you could, the sooner the better. We need to build a timeline of where they travelled to after leaving this petrol station. Take Ty with you."

Karen left her team to it while she headed back to her office.

19

KAREN CLOSED the door to her office, sat in her seat, and buried her head in her hands. Her room felt stuffy, and the heat pressed against her chest. By the end of the day, the heating in the building made it feel suffocating. The day hadn't really started, and a thumping headache brewed. "What do I do?" she murmured.

She had two women missing and no idea where they were. Were they still in the York area or did they get taken elsewhere? She shook her head; the idea wasn't even worth contemplating. The landscape surrounding York was so sparse and remote, it would take an army of hundreds of officers to scour the area properly.

Karen bolted upright as her phone rang. "Shit." She reached for it and saw that it was Owen. Karen cleared her throat and prepared herself for further news. "Owen."

"You sound as bad as I feel," Owen replied.

"The case is getting to me. I could find more clues in a bowl of Heinz Alphabet spaghetti. Shit isn't it?"

"Yep. I can't tell you how much pressure we are under here. We're getting so much flack and grief from the families. We have a news team camped outside our station, and the parents of Raveena and Louisa contact my team daily despite having a FLO assigned to each family."

Karen shook her head and closed her eyes. She sympathised with Owen and his team despite thinking she had it bad. "This is a shitstorm."

"Tell me you've got good news that I can pass on to the families?" Owen fell silent for a few moments. "Anything."

"Okay, we have found nothing from the call logs or the socials. But following our appeals, we've recovered CCTV footage from a petrol station five miles from Yearsley Woods." Karen covered the details with Owen.

"That's promising."

"It is. I've instructed my team to look for more CCTV or doorbell footage from along that road. I don't think there's much along that stretch to be honest."

"Well, it's something, I guess, and I can relay that to the families," Owen added.

Karen sensed the disappointment in Owen's voice. "I'm really sorry, Owen. We are trying our hardest. I can't be certain that Raveena and Louisa are still in the area."

"Don't say that."

Karen changed direction. "Have you located Karim yet?"

"No. We have had officers going door to door and talking to his associates, but they've hit a wall of silence."

"Sounds like he's guilty of something, or...?" Karen trailed off.

"I don't know. We're not his number-one fan, and he has received cautions, arrests, and charges multiple times. He can smell us a mile off and has far too many associates to set alarm bells ringing each time we pull up on the estate. By then he's long gone. It's happened before, and it's happening again."

"Have you tracked down his location using his phone?"

"There is a number for him, however, the cell site analysis has verified that the number's location has remained unchanged in the past two weeks. We've been to the address; it's his mum's place. From our past run-ins, he owns several phones, so my guess is he's using a burner or two."

Stands to reason, Karen thought.

"We had another vigil in town last night. High profile this time with the local MP in attendance. Let's just say he was quite vocal about our efforts, and not in a positive way."

Karen grimaced. She imagined how she would feel if it were happening on her doorstep. Karen leant back into her chair and rocked back and forth. She listened as Owen continued to give her further updates on their enquiries in and around Swansea. After he finished, they fell silent for a few moments, both without anything to say.

Pulling herself upright, Karen stretched her back to ease the soreness. "Okay, Owen, I need to head back out. We're looking for a hermit who lives in Yearsley Woods. Been there his whole adult life. Since Georgia was found in the woods, I hope he may have seen or heard something."

"Not a suspect?"

Karen dismissed the idea, telling Owen that with no transport, it would be impossible for Charles to move round the three different locations unless he had help. She cut the call not long after, agreeing to talk again during the next twenty-four hours.

20

KAREN PICKED up Dan after the call with Owen and made her way towards Yearsley Woods again. The thought crossed her mind as to why she was putting in so much effort to search for a hermit, but she soon countered the argument in her head with the necessity to ensure that she pursued every lead or opportunity. She knew for many years of policing that ninety-nine per cent of the leads that they followed up on would result in a dead end. It was that one per cent that every officer clung to that pushed her to find the Yearsley hermit.

"Time is running out for us, isn't it?" Dan stared at the winding country road ahead.

Karen pursed her lips and nodded. "It feels that way. The PolSA team checked in this morning and found nothing new in the area where Georgia was found. NPAS also guided the team to three different locations near Pickering. Again nothing."

"Do you think Claire will find anything in her search of properties close to the petrol station?"

"I hope so. It's the only credible sighting of all three

women before their disappearance. I imagine dozens of vehicles passed them and recorded the Astra but were oblivious to it."

The more Karen listened to herself, the more hopeless the situation sounded. Forensics were still working to find a match for the tyre tracks discovered close to where Georgia was found. Though each individual lead appeared inconsequential, Karen had experienced cases where many of them all fell into place after arresting a suspect. That meant little to her now, because Raveena and Louisa were out there somewhere.

"This is a nightmare," Dan mumbled.

Karen sensed the despondency in his tone. She glanced over to her left to see Dan stare out of his passenger window.

"Hey, we have to stay positive. The team could uncover a vital piece of evidence right now which would blow this case wide open. That's what we need to hang on to."

"Yeah, I know." Dan pulled a Gorilla bar from his pocket and undid the wrapper. "Want half? Cookies and cream. Packed with protein."

Karen shook her head. It sounded delicious. "You've been packing in the protein again. Are you thinking of competing? I saw you neck a protein shake before we left."

Dan was a powerful and muscular man, with a back as wide as a door, and biceps the size of breeze blocks. Sometimes Karen wondered if he even had a neck because his shoulders were so thick. He attended the gym five days a week and had competed in bodybuilding competitions.

Dan wiped his mouth. "Thinking about it. I love them. The bulking phase was good because I could eat six thousand calories a day, but it was the cutting phase I found the hardest."

"Six thousand calories!" Karen's eyes widened in

shock. "Can you imagine the amount of cheesecake you can devour without any guilt?"

Dan laughed. "I'm not sure cheesecake is on the menu when you're bulking. It's more about having six enormous meals a day. A shit ton of carbs, lean meats, and fish, and bulking shakes."

Karen pulled a face. "In that case, sod that."

They pulled up in the same spot as last night, stepped out of the car, and put on their wellington boots again before heading to the hermit camp. The woods had a different feel during the day. They felt free and open, a natural wilderness that blended in to the lush green countryside. Here for hundreds of years, it had remained untouched by human inhabitation.

Belinda's comments about old folklore brought a smile to her face as she and Dan weaved in between the trees, approaching the den in silence, watching their every step to make sure they didn't alert him. She prayed the hermit was there this time because she wasn't sure if they would ever find him.

The smell of burning wood tickled her nostrils, and she gave Dan a knowing look. They were close, and through the trees she could see a hazy billow of smoke lazily climbing towards the sky. Karen slowed her pace. The last few yards took forever. Dan tapped her on the arm and pointed over towards the left-hand side of the camp. She spotted the outline of a body beneath a blanket. Her breath quickened as they inched closer.

There were feet away when the blanket moved, and a figure scurried out from beneath it. The man, wide-eyed and panicked, backed away. He glanced at both of them.

Karen and Dan held up their hands.

"Charles, there's nothing to worry about. We are both police officers. I'm Karen, and this is Dan. I would like to

talk to you. You are Charles?" Karen asked for clarification.

A nervous stand-off continued for a few moments; the
man's movements were jittery as he moved round on the
spot.

"Charles?" Karen asked again. "I promise you. A few
questions and we'll be on our way and leave you in
peace." Karen studied the man for a few seconds before
Charles nodded in response. He had brown matted hair
down to his shoulders, an unkempt beard of the same
colour, and he wore a brown jumper, green padded coat,
khaki combat trousers, and an old pair of army boots.
Karen witnessed the harsh toll that the years had taken on
him. According to the ranger, Charles was thirty-three, but
he looked in his fifties, with thin and weathered features.

"You shouldn't be here. This is my home, and you
need to go," Charles finally said, his voice flat and
demanding.

"You're a hard person to find. We came by last night
and must have missed you."

"I know, I watched you from the trees. During the
night, I forage and hunt."

Karen suspected Charles wasn't far away when they
had visited.

"Why were you hiding from us?" she asked.

"Because I don't talk to people. I don't trust them. This
is my home. My home!" Charles shouted.

Karen raised a hand to pacify the man. "I know. I'm
investigating the discovery of the female body in these
woods a few days ago."

Charles took a step back and shook his head. "I didn't
hurt anyone."

"I didn't say you did. As you rightly pointed out, these
woods are your home. No one else lives round here. I was

hoping you might have heard or seen something. Maybe the sound of a car engine close by, or perhaps saw a man carrying a large bundle through the trees under the cover of darkness?"

"No." Charles moved from the spot he had been rooted to. He stepped towards the fire and opened a bag, pulling a dead rabbit from it.

Karen shot Dan a look of surprise. His expression was the same as they stood and watched Charles skin the animal in front of them.

"My breakfast, lunch, and dinner for today. Do you want some?" Charles asked, not looking up from his work.

Karen thanked him and turned down his offer. "I understand you've lived in these woods for a long time. You must have seen a lot of things happen?"

Charles shrugged. "Not really. I keep myself to myself and rarely see anybody. There are people on bicycles and horses that come through the woods, but they know I live here, so they stay away. We don't bother each other."

"Don't you ever get lonely?" Dan asked, staring at the dissected pieces of meat that were lined up on a log.

"Not really. I've seen what people are like. Greed, power, and the way they hurt people to get what they want."

Karen nodded. It sounded like a reference to his family.

"Are you positive you didn't hear the rumble of a car engine at night while you were out foraging? Maybe headlights in the middle of the woods. Perhaps even the sound of screaming?"

"No. Who was she?" Charles asked, his voice softening, but still not meeting Karen's eye.

"Someone who had gone camping with two friends. Her two friends are missing."

"Sorry."

"Yeah, so are we. Listen, as part of the elimination process, I need to take a buccal swab from you. There's no need to worry, it doesn't mean you're in any trouble. By taking a simple swab from the inside of your mouth, we can cross-reference it against any evidence we find. It will help us eliminate you from our enquiries."

Charles shook his head in defiance. And for the first time in this conversation, he raised his eyes and narrowed them towards Karen.

"Please. It will take a few seconds, and then we'll be on our way. I'd prefer to do this nicely."

Five minutes later, Karen and Dan headed back to their cars, a buccal swab sample in Karen's handbag.

"Suspect?" Dan asked as he pulled the seat belt across his chest.

Karen started the car and pulled off the verge. "Everyone is a suspect. Let's grab some food."

21

K<small>AREN</small> <small>STOPPED</small> at a small café on her way back. Known as the Travellers Retreat, it gave off an impression of being small and cosy as she and Dan entered. The silence outside quickly turned into the noise of mixed conversations bouncing off the walls. Most of the tables were taken, but Dan quickly spotted one towards the back of the café and headed straight for it. His enormous frame drew stares of curiosity.

"This do?" Dan stood beside it and rested his hand on the back of one chair as Karen caught up.

"Works for me." Karen pulled one of the small plastic chairs out and took a seat. She scanned her surroundings. Nothing fancy. Functional. A dozen tables, cheap plastic seats, and a tacky print on the wood-panelled walls. A small glass counter to the back gave customers an opportunity to see what was available.

Karen picked up the laminated menu and cast her eye over the offerings. Cakes, home-made sandwiches, hot drinks, and a few soft drinks.

"Blimey, we're spoilt for choice." Dan averted his eyes

from the menu and looked at Karen and tried his hardest not to laugh.

Karen agreed, but looking round at the customers, the café served its purpose. She could spot the walkers a mile away. Fat walking socks sticking over the top of walking boots, garishly loud waterproof jackets, and small rucksacks tucked under the table. Many of the diners were discussing route options on their maps or checking their phones while they decided where to head off next. She imagined most wanted a cuppa, a quick sandwich, and a trip to the loo before heading off again.

The waitress came over and jotted down their order before disappearing into the kitchen behind the counter. She returned a few minutes later with a cheap plastic tray. "Two ham sandwiches and two cups of tea," the young waitress said, her voice flat and dry. She exuded so little interest and enthusiasm, Karen wondered why she was doing the job.

Karen took a bite of her sandwich, chewed a few times and then tried to swallow. She looked at Dan, who looked equally unimpressed. "The bloody bread is stale," Karen whispered. She took a sip of tea to dislodge the congealed dough lodged in her throat. "I wish I'd had a bit of your Gorilla bar now."

Dan separated his sandwich and picked out the slices of ham to eat. He rested a slice of bread on its thin side. "That's how stale it is. It stands up on its own," he said.

Five minutes later, Karen paid the bill and left, unimpressed with both the service and the quality of the food. "I'll order us a takeaway when we get back to the station." Karen unlocked the car and slid into the driver's seat. She was about to pull away when her phone rang. Her face scrunched up when she saw the caller ID. "Brad? This is a surprise. How are you doing?"

Brad was one of the DCs on her team while at the Met, and someone she hadn't spoken to since leaving London. Karen put the phone on loudspeaker.

"Hi, Karen. I'm good thanks. How are you?"

"I'm doing okay. I've just been to the most godawful café while out on enquiries and I'm hungrier than when I went in there."

"Right, that doesn't sound too good."

"Is this a social call, Brad?"

Brad cleared his throat, and an awkward silence filled the space between them. "Um... Got some bad news. It's McQueen."

Karen's heart thumped in her chest as she stared out of the windscreen as everything else washed from her mind. It was the phone call that none of them ever wanted to hear. "What's... happened?"

"Steve was in an RTC with a van. He was travelling on his motorbike. It's bad."

Karen's heart lurched. A flurry of scenarios rushed through her mind. Steve Nugent had two passions in life, his motorbike and his car. She had seen his bike often, but only seen his car once. It was his pride and joy. He had a genuine Mustang, the exact model that Steve McQueen had driven. She couldn't remember much of the detail, but the words *Bullitt* and Highland Green sprung to mind. With his charming looks, blue eyes, and dapper suits, he looked like a young Steve McQueen, and the nickname McQueen stuck.

Brad continued. "It was a hit and run. He's critical and on life support."

Karen closed her eyes to stop the tears from escaping. It seemed as if time had stopped. "What injuries has he sustained?" she asked, her voice cracking.

"It would be easier to tell you what injuries he *doesn't*

have. Christ, Karen, he's in a bad way. His family has been called to the hospital. He's suffered a right femur break in two places. Right tibia and fibula broken in three places, swelling of the brain, a punctured lung, broken collar bone, fractured skull and right eye socket. He's also got a few cracked ribs, and a left humerus break."

"Shit." Karen turned to look at Dan, who hung his head in shock.

"I can't believe this. I'm..." Karen was at a loss for words as she processed the news.

"I know. We're all in shock. It's hit us hard." Brad let out a heavy sigh. "Anyway, I thought you should know."

Karen swallowed down the upset which threatened to choke off her voice. "Thanks, Brad. Keep in touch and call me as soon as you have any further updates."

Brad hung up. Karen sat in silence; her stare fixed off into the distance.

"You okay?" Dan asked.

Karen nodded before returning to her phone and dialling Jade's number.

"Hi, Karen. How are you getting on? Did you find our elusive hermit?"

"Yes," Karen said solemnly. "Jade, I've got some bad news. McQueen's been involved in an RTC hit and run. He's on life support."

"Oh no. Oh my God." Jade's voice cracked. "Shit."

"I'll see you soon. I'm on my way back." Karen hung up and pulled away at speed, her wheels slipping and squealing on the tarmac.

22

DAN HEADED BACK to the main SCU floor while Karen returned to her office. She hung her coat up, set her bag down beside her desk, and dropped into her seat. So many questions ran through her mind. She shook her head in denial and covered her mouth with her palm.

Moments later, Jade appeared in her doorway chewing on her lip and clutching a scrunched-up tissue in one hand. Karen noticed the red lattice of veins in Jade's eye and stood up and came round to give Jade a hug.

"I can't believe it," Jade muttered.

"Me neither." Karen returned to her side of the desk and updated Jade on her call with Brad. Jade gasped as Karen recalled Steve's injuries. Her news set off Jade again as more tears flowed.

Karen's team back in London were tight. Not just work colleagues, but friends, people who you would trust with your life. That's why it hurt so much to hear the news. Her thoughts drifted back to happier times in London. Steve was a cheeky chappie with a million-dollar smile who turned heads wherever he went. He was never short of female admirers. Karen always thought he could have made it as a male model for one of the men's fashion houses because of his impeccable dress sense.

At times she had experienced a hot flush beside him and remembered a visit to an ex-con called Dean Macholl. Macholl had offered her and Steve a seat on his small couch, and as they'd sat, the worn cushions had led to them sliding into one another. She smiled at the memory.

"He's a fighter. Steve will pull through," she said to reassure Jade, but doubted her own words as they left her lips.

Jade sniffed and dabbed her eyes. "Why? Steve wouldn't harm a fly. How could some idiot driver do this?"

Karen shrugged. "Wrong place, wrong time. It's a common problem in London. Dangerous driving, too many vehicles on the road, and everyone in a hurry. In Steve's case, Brad mentioned that it was a stolen van."

"Bastards," Jade muttered.

It was rare to hear Jade swear, so Karen knew how much this was affecting her. In that moment, Karen jumped up from her chair to Jade's surprise. "I need to have a word with the super. Back in a jiffy."

KELLY WAS at her desk reviewing papers when Karen knocked on the closed door. "Come!" Kelly shouted.

Karen opened the door halfway and poked her head round the corner. "Ma'am, can I have a quick word?"

"Sure, come in. What's up?"

Karen stepped into Kelly's office and experienced the wall of suffocating heat. She thought her office was hot, but Kelly's was tropical. The heating system was going berserk.

Kelly placed her pen on her desk and interlocked her fingers on the desk. She greeted Karen with a small smile.

"Ma'am. I've got a personal issue. Steve Nugent, one of my old DCs from my Met team was involved in a RTC while riding his motorbike. A stolen van collided with him."

Kelly's face took on a serious expression as she nodded. "I'm sorry to hear that."

"He's critical and on life support." Karen braced herself before she continued. "I know we're in the middle of a major investigation, but can I ask for myself and Jade to make a flying visit to London? There's a strong risk he will not make it and we'd like to see him one last time."

Kelly pursed her lips and studied Karen, but before Kelly could reply, Karen continued.

"It would only be for a few hours. I'd be back later this evening and I'll leave Belinda as acting SIO in my absence. And, if there are any major developments, I'll turn round and head right back." Karen paused for a second, feeling relieved to have got it all out. She'd run through what to say as she made her way to Kelly's office, but wasn't sure how it would go down. "I know it's a lot to ask, but we'd like to see him and say our goodbyes. His family has been called in for that same reason."

Kelly unlocked her fingers and rapped her nails on her desk. Her eyes danced round the room as she weighed up Karen's request. "It's a big ask, Karen, and to have both of you out of the office during such a crucial time is leaving us vulnerable, me included."

"I appreciate that."

It appeared like ages before Kelly spoke again.

"Okay. Go. Keep it quick, keep your phones on, and don't hang around. Understood?"

"Yes, ma'am. Thank you. We'll leave now."

Karen rushed back to her room to find Jade still there nursing her damp tissue, which was in bits on her lap.

"Jade, get your coat. We're going to see Steve now."

Jade looked up in shock, her mouth open, her eyes wide. "What?"

"Go. Grab your coat and meet me in the car park," Karen said, logging off her PC and grabbing her coat, bag, and keys. "I'll brief Bel before I leave."

23

It was late afternoon by the time Karen pulled into the North Middlesex University Hospital car park. For a change, Karen welcomed the fact that finding a space wasn't a problem, as their journey from York had been filled with reflection. They both spoke of Steve and their time in London, and it felt strange being back here.

Smells of disinfectant, coffee, and cooked food wafted round them as Karen and Jade entered the bright, impressive, and gleaming reception area. She'd not visited this hospital during her time with the Met, and it appeared clean and modern.

Jade asked for directions from the reception team, and before long they were up a floor and heading towards the critical care unit. It wasn't long before Karen spotted Brad slouched forward in a chair, his elbows resting on his thighs, and his hands clasped together as if in prayer. Upon hearing their footsteps, he glanced up and rose to his feet, a look of surprise in his eyes as he greeted them.

"I had no idea you were coming."

Karen smiled. "We didn't know ourselves until a few

hours ago. We're in the middle of a major investigation, but we had to come... in case..." Karen didn't want to finish her sentence. It felt too final if she did. "Any news?"

Brad shook his head. "His family came this morning. Awful." Brad lowered his head. "They were all crying. It set me off again. The doctors have given him a twenty per cent chance of pulling through."

"What do we know about the van?" Karen asked.

"A white Fiat Ducato, twenty plate. Stolen in Balham three nights before the accident. Found burnt out three miles from the scene. Forensics were doubtful whether they could recover anything of significance."

Karen doubted it was joyriders. Vehicle thefts had been on the rise in the London area. There had been a shift from car theft to commercial vehicle thefts. "Who was the vehicle registered to?"

"A local builder," Brad replied. "Officers believe someone stole it for its tools and equipment. The wreck was empty once the fire service brought the fire under control."

"Can we go in?" Jade asked.

"Yes, there's no strict visiting hours. You'll have a view of him through a glass window."

Karen rubbed Brad's arm and headed for the double doors, stopping for a brief second to apply hand sanitiser. Jade followed behind and furiously pumped away on the jar until her hands were dripping with the goo. The sound of bleeping monitors greeted them. To the far end of the corridor was a small ward with six beds, each with a patient surrounded by a bank of monitors and machines. Nurses moved silently round the ward checking on their patients. On each side of the corridor were small, one-bed rooms with patients hooked up to the same equipment. Karen and Jade walked side by side, glancing in the rooms on their respective sides until Jade elbowed Karen in the ribs.

"Shit," Karen whispered as they stopped by a glass window. It took her breath away as Karen stared at the broken form lying in a bed, an oxygen tube down their throat, and wires trailing from beneath the bedcovers to the equipment close by. Steve Nugent was unrecognisable. Tears filled her eyes. She heard Jade sniff beside her. A swollen face replaced his boyish good looks, with puffy, bloodied eyelids, and deep cuts and grazes to his skin. His head was almost twice as large as normal. Steve was in a bad way. Various casts supported his broken limbs, and as Karen stood there, she wondered how bad his internal injuries were.

"Oh my God, I can't believe this has happened," Jade said, her voice breaking.

Karen nodded. A twenty per cent chance of recovery. Tight odds. She was overwhelmed by a feeling of help-lessness while standing there. If only she could do more. She willed him to get better.

"Are you okay?" Karen placed her arm round Jade's shoulder.

"I don't know. I want him better, and I want the fuckers who did this found."

They stood in silence staring at Steve's body. Karen wanted to go in and hold his hand in case she didn't see him again.

"Did you know that Steve asked me out once?" Jade said.

Karen glanced over at Jade; her brow pinched in the middle. "Really?"

Jade looked straight ahead. "Don't sound so surprised. I'm not that much of a moose."

Jade's comment brought a smile to Karen's face.

"And he wasn't drunk. Steve's got good taste," Jade added.

"Well, you're off the market now anyway, so Steve missed out. Come on, let's grab a coffee and catch up with Brad. I can't watch."

———

BRAD CUPPED his coffee in his hands and stared down at the table. Jade sat beside him, and Karen opposite. The café was busy. Visitors sat with patients, and hospital staff filtered in during their breaks to get refreshments.

"It's good to see you, Brad," Karen said. "It's a shame that such a tragic accident led to us being here."

"I know. And it's good to see you both too." Tears rolled down from Brad's eyes and dripped off his cheeks.

Karen squeezed his arm. "Brad, we need to stay optimistic. Steve is a fighter. He will pull through. He won't be in a hurry to leave his fancy suits or his classic car."

Brad smiled. "It's sad to see him like that."

Karen leant forward and rested her elbows on the table. She glanced round and lowered her voice. "The investigating team must have recovered CCTV footage to build a timeline of the incident up to where the van was set on fire?"

"They have," Brad replied. "They're gathering more footage closer to where the van was dumped. A resident of the street heard it brake and saw two white males exit before setting it alight. They escaped in a black Audi A6 waiting nearby."

The news piqued Karen's interest, and she was about to say something when she recognised other officers arriving through the main reception area. *Former colleagues of Steve.* "Listen, we need to head back. You hang on in there and thank you for being here for Steve. Can you update me if there's any change in his condition? Or any developments in his case?"

"Of course. Have a safe journey back."

Karen and Jade left Brad looking like a broken soul as they headed back to the car park. Though she didn't want to entertain the idea, Karen reflected on whether this would be the last time she saw Steve alive.

24

A SMILE FORMED on the man's face as he hunched over his laptop. His breath slipped from his mouth in little white clouds as an icy chill sent his body into an involuntary shiver.

He'd held off killing the Asian one for a few days because the bids and requests were so strong. His eyes scanned the list of requests in both surprise and shock at the depravity of his audience. *I wonder what they do in their normal lives?* he thought. Through years of making contacts online, he knew many had normal lives, and kept their darkest secrets locked away from their families. He'd spoken to lawyers, doctors, mechanics, postmen, even those connected in political circles both here in the UK and the US. From those earning a basic wage to the rich and wealthy who saw this as nothing more than an extreme version of going to the casino and blowing thousands of dollars on a hunch or desire to win.

The usual punters were online, pledging eye-watering amounts hoping their bid was the highest and their request was the one he picked to deliver on their behalf.

The Saudi bidder was there tonight. His current bid stood at eleven grand. The man believed he was connected to royalty because part of his username included the word prince.

The man typed a reply to prince49189 who had expressed a particular interest in Raveena.

You'll have to do better than your 11K. She's dark-skinned, slender, and ripe. You've seen how pathetic she is. If you want more, you pay more.

Prince49189 didn't reply straight away, so the man carried on scrolling through the bids and requests. There was a flutter in his stomach and an eagerness to get on as he typed out another message to his audience. Tonight was the night, and he needed to close the vote.

Two minutes to get your vote and pledges in.

A last glance between Raveena and Louisa on the live feeds, and then he hit the stop button. He nodded in agreement. The next victim had been chosen, and the pledges had exceeded those of Georgia. This would be savage.

With the white plastic sheet down, wooden chair in the middle, and cable ties lying close by on the floor, the scene was set. Before heading off to the cells, he checked the camera on the nearby tripod to make sure it was connected to the live feed. The keys jangled in his hand, the metallic sound echoing in the space. Unlocking the door, the light from behind him illuminated the dark space. He took a deep breath and entered.

Raveena gasped and pushed back with her heels, the

whites of her wide eyes staring at him in sheer terror as she mumbled.

"It's your turn," he said striding towards her and grabbing her by the neck of her T-shirt. Her arms flailed as she fought to push away his hands. "Fight as much as you want," he said through gritted teeth. "You'll make me a rich man."

Her chin trembled as she squeezed her eyes shut, her whole body shaking with tremors. "Please, I don't want to die. Please let me go," Raveena screeched. Spittle erupted from her mouth. Against the force of his powerful arms, she retreated into a foetal position, covering her face and tensing her muscles into a rigid posture.

The man raised his hand and slapped her hard across the back of her head. The thwack echoed round the room. He stooped and grabbed at her limbs. They were sweaty and clammy, but that wouldn't deter him. She fought harder, pulling her knees up to her chest and kicking him away. "Bitch!" he shouted. Not happy with her defiance, he caught her ankles and dragged her from her cell, her hands clutching at the floor, hoping to find something to slow her down. The bright arc lights blinded her, which added to her confusion as she stared at her new surroundings.

Fed up with her antics, he curled his hand into a fist and punched Raveena hard across the face, dazing her as she screamed. The blow bought him enough time to loop his arms round her waist and hoist her up on to the chair. He tied her wrists and ankles to the frame of the chair with long, black cable ties. Though in pain, Raveena thrashed in the chair. A mix of blood, sweat, and tears formed a sticky goo, which dribbled down her cheeks and off her chin.

The man checked the comments flooding in on the

live stream. He had whipped them into a frenzy, which made him smile. With one last glance at the screen, he began his work. A volley of punches to her face and abdomen. Each one set off a spasm of pain. Raveena flinched and convulsed as she groaned. He picked up the scissors from the table and cut away at her clothes, tearing them to shreds until she was naked. Her firm, pert breasts now resembled something from a horror movie as trickles of blood snaked their way down her chest.

Raveena's swollen and battered face hung low, a few groans telling him she was still conscious. Next, it was a turn for his trusted pair of pliers. He grabbed Raveena's hair and yanked her head back, holding her in place while he forced the nose of his pliers between her tight lips. Raveena groaned again and wriggled, but he was too strong as her lips tore and the nose of the pliers disappeared inside her mouth. He felt round and clamped the serrated edges on the tip of her tongue before pulling it out. Letting go of her hair, he reached for his scissors again and cut off her tongue close to her teeth. A two-inch stub of flesh hung from the jaws of his pliers. He tossed the bit to the floor.

That was worth twenty grand.

He continued torturing her for the next twenty minutes, delivering on the pledges. One by one he cut off her fingers and slashed at her torso, before pulling her legs apart and carrying out the last request which had come with a twenty-two grand pledge. Though Raveena was semi-conscious, her body spasmed and twitched as it fought for relief from the pain. The violence continued for a short while until he grabbed his club, took a wild swing and delivered a final blow to her head that stilled her body.

He grabbed a towel and wiped the blood from his

hands as he checked his laptop. The event had proved successful. Now it was time to put Raveena out of her misery for good. With a knife in one hand, he gripped her thigh and pressed the tip of the blade in, giving it a wiggle before pulling it out. A steady stream of blood poured from the wound as he took a step back and watched her slip away over the next few minutes.

With the final involuntary twitch of nerve impulses in her body, the live event ended. He switched the feed and left his audience to watch Louisa's body curl up into a ball within her cell, her sobs coming through the walls.

Now began the clear-up operation. Under the cover of darkness, he would dispose of Raveena's body and clear up tomorrow morning.

25

KAREN COMBED her fingers through her wet hair as she sat at the dining table chewing on a piece of toast. Zac had woken earlier than her, bringing up a cup of tea for her in bed before she'd showered and joined him downstairs. He had rustled up scrambled eggs on toast for them and they'd taken the opportunity to catch up over breakfast. It had been a late one by the time Karen had arrived back in York. She'd dropped Jade at the station so she could collect her car before heading to Zac's. He'd been dozing in bed as she'd walked through the door, and though they'd talked about her visit to see Steve, Karen had needed sleep.

Zac looked at Karen over the top of his coffee mug. "How are you doing today?" He placed his mug down and chased a few remaining bits of scrambled egg round his plate with his fork.

Karen wasn't sure how to answer. She was pleased to have been to London in case Steve didn't make it. But felt shocked and saddened at the severity of his injuries.

"The doctors have given him a twenty per cent chance of pulling through."

Zac stared at her wide-eyed as his jaw dropped. "Let's hope they find the people responsible. They should be able to gather enough information to create detailed profiles of the two suspects who ran from the van."

Karen hoped so. With it being a residential street, there was a strong probability that investigating officers could find CCTV or Ring doorbell footage from houses close to the scene.

"If Steve doesn't make it, and I pray he does, would you go to the funeral?"

Karen nodded as she took a sip of her tea.

"Would you like me to come with you? I know you'll be going with Jade, but I didn't know if you'd like me to come as well?"

Karen offered Zac a small smile and reached out and squeezed his hand. "I think that would be nice."

They both fell silent as they heard the thunder of footsteps. Summer appeared in the kitchen doorway with sleepy eyes, her hair a bedraggled mess, and wearing crumpled pink pyjamas. Her bare feet slapped on the kitchen floor.

She yawned before heading for the fridge to fetch the milk for her cereal.

"Morning, sleepyhead. Are you okay?" Zac asked.

"Hmmm," Summer replied.

Zac raised a brow in Karen's direction.

"Make sure you're not late for school," Zac said.

"Hmmm," Summer replied again, her voice rough and gravelly, and typical of a moody teen first thing in the morning.

They watched as she prepared a bowl of cereal and stomped back upstairs ignoring them. Zac blew out his cheeks. "That was a barrel of laughs," he commented with a chuckle.

Karen stood. "I need to dry my hair before I leave, so I'll pop in and see her." She rose from her chair and gave Zac a kiss on top of his head before heading upstairs.

Summer sat on the edge of her bed, cereal bowl on her lap, spoon in one hand, her phone in the other. *Yep, typical teenager.* Karen tapped on the open door. "Room for one more?"

Summer nodded and forced a weak smile.

"You okay?" Karen asked.

Summer swallowed her mouthful of Rice Krispies before replying. "Yeah. Tired. I was chatting with friends late last night on Snapchat. Dad is always too cheerful in the morning."

Karen nudged Summer with her shoulder. "He loves you. We both do. I guess he's eager to see you first thing in the morning."

Summer rolled her eyes.

Karen looked round Summer's room. A typical teenager's den. Clothes strewn across the floor. Empty Coke cans on her desk. An overflowing make-up bag by her mirror, and a stale lingering smell because teenagers never opened their windows for fresh air.

"Hey, I was thinking it's been a while since the three of us went out for dinner. How about we go tonight? My shout and your choice of restaurant? What do you say?"

Karen noticed Summer's eyes twitch a bit and her hesitancy to reply. It was clear to Karen that the horrible experience at the hands of Harmans' mob played on Summer's mind. According to Zac, Summer wasn't going out much and rarely ventured out by herself.

"I don't mind." Summer shrugged a shoulder.

"Well, I think it would be nice. It's been a while since I

spent time with you. I'll square it up with your dad, and I'll see you this evening." Karen squeezed Summer's knee before she stood and left the room. She was on the upstairs landing when Zac shouted up to her.

"Your phone is ringing. It's Ed."

Karen turned and shuffled down the stairs as quick as she could, half jogging into the kitchen to grab her phone from the worktop. "Ed, hello there."

"Morning, Karen. Bad news I'm afraid. We've been called out to the discovery of a body. An Asian female."

Karen closed her eyes as dread and regret washed over her. She felt a heaviness press against her chest as she let out a long sigh. "Raveena?"

"I don't know, but more than likely. All I've got is a naked, young Asian female."

Gut instinct told her it was Raveena. Time had run out. "Where?"

"York golf club. I'll send you the details and see you there."

Karen cut the call and turned to Zac. He didn't need to say anything. It was evident to both of them that the case had taken another bad turn.

26

QUESTIONS TUMBLED through Karen's mind until it felt like her brain was about to explode. There had been no reports of any missing person of Asian descent in the last few days other than Raveena. It had to be her. If it was, it would be hard to accept. But the doubt was there in her mind. Had they missed vital clues? Had they searched the wrong areas? Another family who was about to receive devastating news, and it was that thought which made her slap the steering wheel. It would be another uncomfortable call with Owen and a difficult visit for his officers.

Police tape sealed off Lord's Moor Lane outside of York golf club. The clubhouse and car park were to her left. The course was on the opposite side of the road to her right. Karen slowed her car and held up her card towards the police officer manning the outer cordon. He nodded before lifting the tape and waving her through. She thanked him and travelled a further hundred yards until she spotted Ed in the middle of the road pointing towards a turn-off just in front of him. Karen followed his directions and turned into an unmade track which skirted the golf club.

As Karen slowed, she saw further police tape along the track. There wasn't anywhere in particular to park, so Karen pulled up on her left away from the tape, grabbed her handbag, and stepped out of the car, locking it behind her. Ed jogged up the track towards her.

"Have you had a look?" Karen asked.

Ed nodded. "I think it's her."

Karen furrowed her brow. "You think?"

"Yeah. I can't be certain because someone heavily mutilated the body. Much worse than Georgia."

Karen's eyes widened in consternation. She asked Ed to show the way. They cut through a hedge, and Karen found herself on the fairway. She followed Ed towards the white forensic tent set up on the right-hand side of the lush grass.

"When you said York golf club, I didn't think you meant on the course!"

"The fifteenth fairway, to be precise," Ed clarified.

In Karen's opinion, it was remote enough, with a quiet lane off of Lord's Moor Lane where the killer wouldn't be spotted, and then the whole course to choose from.

"We found tyre marks a bit further up the track and grass impressions on that side of the fairway," Ed pointed out. "I think he carried the body from his vehicle and left it further up."

"Is Izzy here?"

"Yes. She's inside the tent. It's not pretty."

"Any eyewitnesses?" Karen stopped by the inner crime cordon to sign into the scene log the scene guard presented to her.

"Your pack, ma'am." The female officer handed Karen a small plastic package. Karen thanked her and tore it open. She placed the blue elastic booties over her shoes and snapped on the blue nitrile gloves.

"Not as yet. One of the groundsmen found her as he drove round checking the greens before the first golfers were due on. It's seniors' day, whatever that means. A dozen golfers were teeing off at nine."

Forensic officers in their white Tyvek suits busied themselves round the tent. Camera footage was being examined, paperwork being completed, and several were on their hands and knees examining the ground round the tent. A line of metal plates provided a safe and sterile entry and exit point to the crime scene.

"Right, let's have a look." Karen peeled back the flap on the tent and stepped in. She stood back and took a moment to take in the scene. The grass round the body had deep impressions, but she imagined much of that was down to the ground staff, forensic team, and the first responding officers. Karen's eyes moved up the victim, starting with her bare feet, then her bloodstained legs and mutilated chest, before ending at her swollen and battered face. It wasn't until the last minute she noticed the victim missing her fingers.

Izzy, who had been quiet until that point, looked up at Karen and shook her head. There was visible distress in her eyes as she let out a heavy breath. "Awful. Bloody awful. Is it one of your missing women?"

Though the woman was almost unrecognisable, there were certain distinctive features like her long black hair, wide set eyes, pointed chin and high cheekbones that suggested it was Raveena. Body characteristics seemed to suggest that as well. Though she would need a formal identification, her hunch was that they had found Raveena. Despite her efforts to look away, her eyes were drawn to the physical injuries and laceration marks across the victim's chest.

"I think so. Cause of death?"

"Looks like blood loss, but there's also a deep injury to the side of her skull, which may have contributed to her death. I'll need to examine it more closely during the PM. She has the same deep wound to her inner thigh as Georgia, so I would say it's the same perp," Izzy replied.

"Eyes intact?"

Izzy nodded. "But she's had her tongue removed. No sign of it."

"What?"

"Yes, cut out. There is a lot of tissue damage to the inside of her cheeks and gums, suggesting that it was forcibly removed. She's also suffered violent trauma to her genitalia. The poor luv put up a fight." Izzy used the tip of her pen to point out further injuries. "Extensive abrasions and bruising to her face, the palms, heels, back, and shoulders. Again, I'll examine them in more detail during the PM."

"He did a right number on her then." Karen sighed and left the tent.

"Savage, right?" Ed said as he joined Karen.

Karen nodded as she rested her hands on her hips and stared off into the distance. The golf course featured long, closely manicured fairways interspersed with pristine, finely cut springy greens that held a soft bounce. She noticed the tops of a few sand bunkers, and water hazards that would swallow a ball forever, scattered among the deep grass known as the rough. It was a very relaxing place to come and spend a few hours, though she had never seen the appeal herself. And yet this calm and pleasant setting had been chosen as the place to dispose of a body. Deliberate or convenient?

"Derek Redmond, the club manager, wants a word with us. He's going bananas. They've got golfers waiting to tee off and he's moaning about the club losing money."

Karen raised a brow. "Bloody muppet. They found the mutilated body of a young woman on his course, and all he's worried about is the club being closed. Prat! Let's have a word with him," Karen fumed as she stormed off with Ed and headed back to the clubhouse.

27

KAREN HEARD the raised voices as she stepped through the doors of the clubhouse. The source of the commotion was clear when she found a group of gentlemen in the middle of an argument. They jabbed accusatory fingers towards one man who was red-faced and flustered, doing his best to pacify them. "We paid to play out there!" "The bloody police can't tell us when we can and can't play!" "This is disgusting!" "Why didn't anyone call us and save us a trip out here?" The verbal volley continued.

Karen looked at Ed, who shrugged. She blew out her cheeks and pulled out her warrant card before pushing through the crowd to stand at the front. "Please! Will you be quiet."

The comments kept flying.

"Shut up!" Karen shouted. "I need you to shut your bloody traps!" Her face turned as red as a tomato as she screamed at the top of her voice. It took a few moments before they all piped down, a few looking at her in disgust as if what right did she have to talk to them in that manner? "Thank you. I'm Detective Chief Inspector Karen Heath of

York police. I'm in charge and it was my decision to close the club for the time being while we investigate a serious crime."

"It doesn't mean we can't play on the other holes. We could easily do a front nine, and skip the back nine," one member shouted.

"It's not happening. We have an active investigation underway because we've discovered a body on the fifteenth fairway. And I'm not prepared to have anyone come close to the scene."

"Just get on with it so that we can get back to playing. This is our regular once a week meet-up for the senior members of the club," an elderly member interjected.

Karen shook her head. "I don't care. I suggest you get back in your cars and my officers will show you the correct way to leave the area. If you choose to stay and interfere with my crime scene, my officers will arrest you for obstruction." Karen saw the look of surprise on many of the member's faces.

"Ridiculous," the man huffed.

Karen stepped towards him, locking eyes with him as she stared him down. "Let me ask you a question. Do you have a daughter?"

The man seemed taken aback by the question. He nodded.

"How old?"

"That's none of your business."

Her jaw stiffened. "How bloody old is she?"

The man tutted. "Twenty-five."

"How would you feel if the body of your twenty-five-year-old daughter had been discovered out there? Would you be happy for me to open up the course so that everyone can pile on and go about their day, or would you want the privacy for your daughter while we did our utmost to gather as much evidence as we could before moving her body in a dignified way away from the public gaze?"

The man swallowed hard and then looked at the sea of faces staring back at him.

Karen raised a brow. "Simple question. How would you feel?"

The man bowed his head and took a step back in defeat, which weakened the resolve of fellow members.

"Right, pack your stuff up and get out of here. I need you all to leave." Karen turned towards the man who had endured their fury. A portly figure with droopy jowls and thin greying hair combed back. He wore black trousers, a smart white shirt, and a navy jumper with the York golf club crest on its chest. "Derek Redmond?"

Redmond nodded, his limbs shaking as he glanced over Karen's shoulder at the club members filtering away. "Please come to my office."

Karen and Ed followed the man along the corridor. To the left and right of them were many club photos of past presidents, team captains, trophies, even the history of the club. Out of the corner of her eye she caught a newspaper clipping which talked about the club being on this site since 1904. *Impressive*, she thought.

Redmond showed them into an office with a large plush table and chairs at one end, and a sofa at the other. A deep red carpet and wood-panelled walls added to the history of the place. "Please, take a seat."

Karen and Ed took a seat opposite him. "Is this going to take long?"

She wanted to tell him to shut up as well, but she needed his cooperation. "As long as it takes." Without giving him the opportunity to say anything else, she carried on, "Do you have any CCTV covering that side of the road?"

"No. But we have CCTV for the clubhouse, main entrance, and the car park outside."

"My officers will need a copy of the footage for the last twenty-four hours. Do the cameras capture anything of the road beyond the car park and main entrance?"

Redmond nodded. "I think so. It captures some of the road beyond it. I suspect it's not as clear though."

"Anything is better than nothing. I'd also like a list of your members."

Redmond flinched and pushed back in his chair. "Sorry? You don't think any of our members had anything to do with this? That's absurd."

"I'm not suggesting that at all. It's a line of enquiry. It would be hard for many people to know about that small unmade track that runs along the back of the course unless you are local to the area. Of course, your members are *very* familiar with the area. I'd like to eliminate as many people as possible from my enquiries."

Redmond shook his head. "Isn't there something about data protection?"

"Yes, but we're dealing with a murder enquiry. If you want to object, that's up to you. But I will come back with a warrant if necessary."

Redmond held out his hands, palms towards Karen. "Okay. Okay. I'll sort that out for you."

"Did anyone report anything suspicious to you in the last twenty-four hours? Anyone lurking? Cars slowing as if looking for something? Vans parked where they shouldn't be?"

"No. Nothing."

Karen asked a few more questions before thanking him and returning to the crime scene.

WHILE ED LIAISED with the crime scene investigators, Karen paced up and down the fairway looking for any breaks in the bushes that formed a barrier between the golf course and the road. Even without their leaves, the hedges were thick and dense. Impossible for anyone to get through them. Knowing it was going to be a tough call, Karen pulled out her phone and called Owen. It was a few seconds before he answered.

"Karen. Any news?"

Karen closed her eyes for a second. "I've got news, but it's not good news. We've got another body. Though it hasn't been formally identified, I'm certain it's Raveena."

"Shit."

Karen took a few moments to give Owen the details on the victim and her injuries. The more she explained, the more horrific it sounded, which left Owen speechless.

"Are you certain it's our man?" he asked.

"Most of the injuries are different. But she's had a few teeth removed against her will, and there's a deep wound to the inside of her thigh. It's in the same spot as Georgia's. Both women died due to blood loss, caused by the same method."

"But the level of violence is on a whole new level. Why?" Owen asked.

"I don't know. It's not uncommon for the level of violence to increase with each victim. I need to find Louisa, because if our last two victims are anything to go by, he's going to put Louisa through hell."

Owen agreed. "I'll warn our FLOs and visit Raveena's parents. Looks like it'll be another visit to York hospital mortuary today."

Sadly, Owen was right. Karen knew with unwavering

certainty that it was Raveena, but she understood the importance of following proper procedure. "Let me know when you get to York, and I'll meet you at the hospital." Karen hung up and dialled Zac's number.

"It's one of your missing women, isn't it?" Zac said, answering his phone, having heard about the discovery through the grapevine.

"Yes. Raveena Chowdhury. The parents are coming down later on today to ID the body. I'm sorry, but we'll have to cancel our dinner tonight with Summer. I know she'll be disappointed, but perhaps we can reschedule it for tomorrow?"

"Of course. I'll let her know when she's back from school, and I'll expect you back late. Let me know if you end up pulling an all-nighter so I can lock the door."

"Will do. Love you."

"Love you too."

Karen stuffed her phone back into her pocket. This was going to be a tough day. Both bodies had been easily discovered. A question rolled round in Karen's mind. Was he bold or careless?

28

KAREN NOTICED a marked shift in the investigation's pace by the time she returned to the station in the afternoon. Much to Derek Redmond's frustration and anger, York golf club would stay closed for the rest of the day while forensic investigations continued. The police dispatched a search team to conduct a detailed sweep of the fairway leading from the unmade track to where the forensic tent was positioned. A private ambulance had taken away the body before Karen left the club. With Ed staying back to oversee the crime scene, Karen hurried back after Belinda had called her with an important update.

Karen made her way through the station, making a pit stop at the canteen to pick up a sandwich and coffee before making her way to the SCU. There was an urgency in her step knowing the team would be at full stretch now with two bodies, one missing person, and a few interesting leads.

"Karen."

It was the unmistakable voice of Kelly. Karen stopped,

fixed a smile, and turned to see her boss catching up with her along the corridor. *More heat.* "Ma'am."

"Good thing I caught up with you. One of our three women?" Kelly asked, ignoring pleasantries and being direct.

"Yes, ma'am. Raveena Chowdhury. Her parents are coming over this afternoon with DCI Lewis for a formal identification, and despite her injuries, it looks like her." Karen took a moment to update her boss on the injuries and the circumstances in which she found her. Kelly grimaced as she listened to the details.

"Not good. Any clues at the scene?"

Karen scratched her nose and shook her head. "Forensics are still at the scene. I've left Ed in charge. The perp is playing with us. I simply know it."

"Why do you say that?"

"The bodies were dumped in a way that did not require much effort to hide them. Okay, the forest doesn't get as much footfall, but a golf club? Dozens of players every day. Right in the middle of the fairway for everyone to see?" Karen paused for a moment before continuing. "It appears he drove into an unmade track that skirts the back of the course. It's off the main road and only used by golfers or ground staff. That's not busy. He could have dumped Raveena there with no one seeing him and driven off again. Why would he park there, and then carry the body a hundred yards up the fairway and leave her there?"

Kelly weighed up Karen's assessment and agreed. "Okay, keep me updated." She paused mid step. "Oh, by the way. Any update on your colleague in London?"

"No, ma'am. He has a twenty per cent chance of pulling through, so I'm glad that Jade and I had the chance to visit him in case it's the last time we see him. Thank you for letting us go."

"Oh, I'm sorry to hear that. That's not good news. It was the right decision for you to go. If you need to talk about it, my door is always open. One other thing. We've had nothing back on Sally Connell from either the NCA or Europol. They are still working on confirming her whereabouts. It might be worth you speaking to your colleagues back in London. Perhaps they can chase up a few of their snouts to see what the word is on the street?"

"Thank you, ma'am. I will do." Karen watched as Kelly turned and strode off down the corridor. Karen continued to the SCU. With her being so consumed in the case, she hadn't thought about Sally Connell.

Karen pushed through the doors of the SCU and made her way straight to the front, a coffee in one hand, a sandwich in the other. She set down the coffee and opened her sandwich packet, taking a large bite because she was starving. The pictures of all three women stared back at her from the whiteboard. Each photo represented a happier time. All smiling, in their prime, with a zest for life. Three intelligent and caring women, and now two dead and one still missing.

She had read up on all three in her own time. They had filled their brief lives with so much. The Duke of Edinburgh's Award was no walk in the park, and yet they had shown courage and perseverance in achieving it. They had spent countless hours visiting local care homes in their neighbourhoods to sit and talk with the elderly residents, hoping to inject frivolity, compassion, and companionship into their lives. Reading all these accounts had saddened her and filled her with so much anger towards the perpetrator.

Belinda joined Karen. "The dashcam footage should be over any moment."

It was the reason Karen had rushed back to the office. Following an appeal for information from the public, holidaymakers from Scotland had come forward to say they believed they'd caught Raveena's car on their dashcam.

While they waited for it to arrive, Karen took a few moments to update the team about the discovery of Raveena Chowdhury's body. As she was finishing a short briefing, Bart Lynch, the CSI manager, appeared through the doors and made his way over to Karen.

"Hi, Karen. I thought I'd update you on the extra resources we pulled in to help us with the trace evidence found on Georgia's body."

"Okay, great. How are you getting on?"

"Pretty good." He passed her the report. "We've had a palynologist use a high-powered microscope to examine the size, shape, and morphology of pollen and spores recovered from the skin. Here's the interesting point, even after washing clothes, pollen can stay in pockets or cuffs, in animal remains or faeces, or in vehicles, packing materials, or any other hard surface, which allows the evidence to be collected long after the incident. Here, the palynologist confirmed that the pollen spores found were not of this year, but of a composition last found three years ago. There was also trace evidence of pollen spores attached to microscopic particles of cow dung."

Karen rubbed her temples. She asked Bart to repeat it while she read the report. After he finished, they both stood in silence while Karen processed the information. She paced round as the cogs in her mind spun at warp speed.

"Christ. It's a disused farm or industrial building that

nobody has used for the past three years. It probably housed farm machinery during its use, which explains industrial grease and cow dung. The wheels of farm vehicles that used the shed, barn, or warehouse might have caused it."

Bart nodded. "It's a place to start."

Before instructing her team, Karen thanked him and then directed them to focus their search on disused farm buildings of any type located between the two points where Georgia and Raveena's bodies had been found.

Belinda waved to Karen to get her attention and shouted across the floor. "The dashcam footage is here."

Karen scooped up her coffee and headed over to Belinda's desk, pulling up a spare chair to sit beside her. It took a few moments for the clip to load. Thankfully, the holidaymakers had only downloaded the clip of Raveena's car. The front of their car appeared in the footage, and it wasn't long before their vehicle passed the black Astra parked up on the side of the road. The car was empty and none of the three women appeared in the footage. Karen sighed.

"Is that it?" she said as the footage continued to play. The view from the car showed a long straight road ahead of them, and a barren wilderness on both sides.

"That's the only sighting of the Astra."

Karen's chest sunk with a disappointment. She had hoped for more. Her eyes widened as she jabbed a finger at the screen. "Stop it there."

Belinda clicked her mouse.

"There!" Karen pointed. Some distance ahead of the car, she noticed a white van parked on the side of the road sitting low in a ditch. "That's an odd place to be? Middle of nowhere."

"Could be walkers. Mountain bikers. It's an easy way to transport your bike, right?" Belinda suggested.

Belinda had a point. Karen made a note of the partial plate. FP09. Bushes hid the rest of the details from view. "Check with the DVLA. Let's see if they can give us a steer on who the vehicle might belong to. See if we can narrow down the make and model."

Having made a note of Karen's request, Belinda let the footage play out to the end. "Anything else you need me to do?"

"Yes. Set up a police notice at this location appealing for any information on a white van." Karen pointed to the timestamp. "And get a few officers to the area to have a look round." Checking the time on her phone, she was running late. "I need to dash. I'm due at the mortuary. Give me an update later." Karen rose from her chair and hurried from the unit.

29

KAREN WHIZZED through the hospital reception and headed for the mortuary. Overseeing the formal identification of a body was one of her least favourite jobs, along with attending the post-mortem. Though the latter helped her do her job and find the clues that would help her bring killers to justice, attending an identification with the loved ones of the deceased always filled Karen with a mixture of deep sadness and grief.

Karen buzzed on the door of the mortuary and waited for one of the mortuary technicians to come and answer the door for her. A minute later, one of Izzy's team, Yvette, answered and stepped to one side.

"Are they here?" Karen asked.

Yvette nodded. "Literally two minutes before you. They are in the relative's room with a family liaison officer and a DCI."

"Okay, thanks. I'll have a word with the DCI first."

Yvette turned and headed back towards the office, leaving Karen to head through on her own.

Karen spotted a man pacing slowly up and down the

corridor. He stopped and looked up when he heard footsteps.

"Owen?"

The man nodded. "Karen?" He extended his hand as Karen approached.

"Yes, good to meet you." Karen shook his hand. He had a strong, muscular grip. He was thickset, with a round chubby face, cropped blonde hair, and metal-rimmed round glasses. She wondered if he played rugby as his broad shoulders and chest appeared to struggle in his suit jacket.

"Sorry it's under these circumstances. How are Raveena's parents?"

Owen grimaced and shook his head. "Her mum cried all the way here. Dad sat stony-faced. He held his wife's hand, but I think he was trying to be strong and brave. But I sensed him buckling at the seams. I thought I would bring along Jacqueline, our FLO appointed to the family. That was a long bloody journey," he said, rubbing the tension from the back of his neck.

"Yes, I can imagine. Long and tense."

"Are they ready for us?" Owen asked.

Karen glanced round but didn't see any staff. "Let me check." She hurried off and headed to Izzy's office. Izzy was busy typing up a report when Karen appeared in her doorway. "Hiya, how's it going?"

Izzy looked up from her screen. "Easy going today. Just the one PM. I thought I would get ahead of myself and get the notes done so I can knock off early."

"Can we do the ID on our second victim? It's probably unbearable for the family sitting in the relative's room."

"Sure. I'll get Yvette to prepare the body and take it to the observation room. Five minutes." Izzy got up from her chair and went in search of Yvette.

While they waited, Owen introduced Karen to Raveena's parents. Raveena's mum barely acknowledged Karen's presence, offering nothing more than a brief nod. The woman's face was flushed and swollen, her eyes bloodshot, and dark circles formed a shadow round them. Involuntary shivers ran down her spine, causing her body to tremble. Raveena's dad stood stony-faced, his shoulders pulled back, his hands clenched into a ball and tucked into his belly. The sleepless nights, the worry, and grief, had left them as nothing more than empty shells.

A few minutes later, another assistant showed Karen, Owen, the FLO, and Raveena's parents to a room next to the observation room. A glass panel separated the two spaces. Yvette stood beside the shrouded body on a gurney. She stared at Karen, who gave her the nod.

Yvette pulled back the shroud and rested it on the shoulders of the body. That was enough for Raveena's mum to let out a screech that tore from her throat before her legs gave way. Jacqueline and Owen rushed forward and caught her just before she collapsed to the floor. Raveena's mum rubbed her chest as she struggled to find her breath. Her lips trembled as she muttered incoherent words. Her shrieks turned to wails as she tossed her head back.

"Can you confirm if that is your daughter, Raveena?" Karen asked the dad, even though from the mother's response suggested it was, procedure needed at least one parent to either nod or verbally confirm the identity.

The dad's eyes flickered as he stared straight ahead before he nodded once. Both Karen and Owen saw his response. Karen looked at Yvette and nodded, who replaced the shroud over Raveena's face. It took a few moments before Karen could usher the parents back into the visitors' room. Once seated, Karen had a few words with Owen before returning to Raveena's parents. She crouched down in front of Raveena's mum.

"I want to say how sorry I am for the loss that you and your family have experienced. I'm the senior investigating officer for York police and I want to reassure you we are doing everything possible to find out who is responsible."

Raveena's mum looked up at Karen, their eyes connecting. In that moment Karen understood the anguish in the woman's eyes... there was no greater pain than that of a parent's grief.

"My daughter," Raveena's mother spat. "You let down my daughter. Why didn't you find her sooner?" Fury tainted her voice as she glared at Karen and then Owen. "I want the person responsible bloody dead."

Karen pursed her lips and glanced at Owen. She stood and turned. She felt her pain and anger. "I'm sorry. Finding all three women has been our priority. I only wish we'd found her sooner too."

Twenty minutes later, and after Raveena's parents felt strong enough to travel, Karen thanked Owen and watched as they left in an unmarked police van, the red rear lights disappearing into the late afternoon darkness. She knew it would be a hard journey back to Swansea filled with more tears, painful memories, and deep reflection.

30

NEEDING to call it a night and go home, Karen left not long after Owen and drove away from the mortuary, her mind awash with so many unanswered questions and a deep-seated ball of sadness. Going to a mortuary was never enjoyable. Being there with parents or relatives of the deceased upset her on so many levels. The reactions she'd witnessed to identifying a body differed in so many ways. Some people would stand there motionless and display no emotion. Others would cry silently. And then there were the ones like Raveena's mum who collapsed and cried hysterically. Each one left an impression in Karen's mind, and showed the fragility that we carried within and an outpouring of grief that knew no limits.

It felt awkward to stand there and impose on such a personal moment, but she was there to do a job. Karen shook her head as she tried to rationalise it in her mind. It hadn't affected her for most of her career. But more recently, she'd noticed a shift in her thinking and reactions. Perhaps Karen attributed it to her age and the realisation that human life was so fragile that it could be taken away in the blink of an eye. When she was younger and early in her career, she'd thought she was indestructible, a force to be reckoned with. But in these emotional moments of late, it didn't seem that way any more. She afforded herself a small smile. Maybe she had matured. The fact of being in a family environment had something to do with it. The loss of her sister had left an enormous gap in her life. Zac and Summer had filled it.

Fifteen minutes into her journey, a glare of headlights bounced off her rear-view mirror and blinded her. Each time they passed over a speed bump, the bright LED beams pierced her eyeballs. Something seemed off. Each time they stopped at lights, the car behind stopped at least two car lengths behind her. That was odd in itself. An overcautious driver?

Karen pulled up at a T-junction and waited for a gap in the traffic before she turned right. The car followed. She continued on her journey with a slight hint of curiosity pricking her thoughts. It was always wise to be cautious, so she took a left taking her further from her route home. A few seconds later, the bright LED head-lights appeared as the car turned down the same street. With her speed remaining constant, Karen traversed a crossroads and proceeded to turn right at the first available chance. She glanced in her rear-view mirror; the car was still there keeping a constant speed and distance between them. It was too dark for her to see the occupant or the make or model of the car. She continued to drive round for a bit, sticking to a few side roads before pulling back out on to a main road again. The following car did the same, slipping in two cars behind.

There was no way she was heading home until she was certain, so she turned off again, moments later to be joined by the same car. By now, she had become convinced that someone was following her. Karen dropped her speed from thirty miles an hour to twenty. The other car did the same, maintaining the distance between them. Karen accelerated away, hitting thirty-five, the pursuing car did the same. Shit.

With her eyes on the road ahead, Karen fumbled round in her handbag searching for her phone. She cursed, annoyed with herself for not connecting her phone via Bluetooth to the car. With her phone in hand, she was about to dial for help when the headlights took a left and disappeared down a side road. Karen narrowed her eyes. She held off calling, but checked each passing side street on her left to make sure that the car wasn't running parallel to her. It was a common tactic she had used as part of a multi-car surveillance operation.

Nothing.

Karen let out a sigh of relief as she placed the phone back in her bag. She hadn't seen the vehicle up close, only as it turned. It was a large black saloon, possibly a Mercedes, Audi, or BMW. Karen's heart hammered in her chest. The threat of Sally Connell being back in the UK had left her on edge, but with her current case, she had taken her eye off the ball. Their mentors had drummed into them at an early stage of their career to always mix up their journeys to and from work. The motto was "repetition leads to mistakes".

Fifteen minutes later and certain she wasn't being followed, Karen pulled up at Zac's and sat in her car for a few minutes, paranoia eating into her. She glanced up and down the road and when certain there was nothing out of the ordinary; she stepped out, locked the car, and hurried into the house.

"Hey, you," Zac said, throwing a tea towel over his

shoulder as he came out of the kitchen to greet her. He noticed the tension in her face. "You, okay?"

Karen pursed her lips and rolled her neck from side to side to relieve the tension. "Yeah. I got spooked coming home. Thought someone was following me." Karen recalled her journey as Zac listened.

"Did you call it in?"

"I was about to, and then the car disappeared." Zac looked over Karen's shoulder towards the front door. She knew what he was thinking. "It's okay. I drove round for a bit to make sure I wasn't being followed, and then I sat outside for a while." Even though it provided a measure of reassurance to Zac, she sensed his worry as he chewed on his bottom lip. After everything that had happened with Summer and her friend, it was understandable that he would feel apprehensive.

"I'll pour you a glass of wine. Are you hungry? I've got leftovers you can have."

"That would be great. I feel bad for letting Summer down. I was looking forward to going out tonight. Is she in her bedroom?"

Zac nodded as he turned and headed back to the kitchen.

Karen headed upstairs and knocked on the bedroom door. "Summer, can I come in?"

"Yeah!" Summer shouted.

Summer was lying on her bed, her legs propped up on the wall, earbuds in her ears. She greeted Karen with a smile and pulled her earbuds out.

Karen dumped herself on the bed beside her and squeezed Summer's shoulder. "What you listening to?"

"Drake." She nodded her head as if replaying the tune in her mind.

"Oooh, good shout. I'm sorry about dinner tonight. I

was looking forward to it. We're great at winding up your dad when we're together." Karen laughed.

Summer laughed and shrugged. "It's okay. I know your work comes first. I'm used to it. Dad's work always got in the way of us spending time together. I think that's why Mum was always mad and drunk by the time Dad got home."

Karen felt a rush of guilt. The job had its demands and would often impact family lives. She'd heard a saying not long after joining the force, "Join the police, get a divorce". Not only were marriages affected, but the kids were too when their parents had to stay late at work or were called in at short notice. Bedtime routines would be disrupted, weekend plans would be postponed, and even school sports days would take a back seat.

"I'm sorry, sweetheart. I'll make it up to you as soon as the case is over." Karen paused and raised a finger. "Sod it. How about dinner tomorrow night?"

"But you're in the middle of a case?"

Karen waved off Summer's concern. "Jade can oversee the case for one evening. Then we can give your dad a hard time. Deal?"

"Deal." Summer's face lit up as she fluffed up her pillow and fell back on to it.

Karen rose from the bed and left Summer to it. She paused in the doorway and watched as Summer put her earbuds back in and mime to the words of a song. Padding back down the stairs, Karen found Zac at the dining table with two glasses of wine and left-over risotto. Now it was time to wind down and relax before having an early night.

31

HE STOOD in the doorway spinning his keys on one finger. Louisa sat paralysed in one corner of her cell, frozen in fear. She didn't glance in his direction, nor did she shrink away like the other two had. He'd listened to her screams while torturing Raveena. He imagined Louisa had experienced every ounce of pain her friend had endured, causing her mind to shut down in order to preserve her remaining sanity.

"IT'S NOT your time yet. But it's coming. I hope you put up a fight. My customers would enjoy it, and I'd earn a shit-load more money." He pulled his shoulders back and let out a breath through his clenched teeth. She'd attempted to reach the bucket but hadn't made it in time. A trail of putrid smelling bile and diarrhoea led to it. Several slices of bread sat in a pile. "You really should try to eat something. After all, you need to keep up your strength. You're going to need it." A sly grin spread across his face as he turned and locked the door behind him, leaving her in darkness once again. He checked the camera feed on his laptop. She remained in the same position. He wondered if she'd be able to move when her time came or if he'd have to drag her out by her ankles.

THE EVIDENCE of Raveena's last moments lay in a bloodied mess on the plastic sheet. Her teeth, the stub of her tongue, the congealed stickiness of her blood, and her fingers. The chair was beyond saving. He would burn the lot in the oil drum outside and set the scene for the next one. Louisa wouldn't be the last. The money he had earned thus far exceeded his wildest expectations. Returning to his laptop, he checked the final total. Forty-three grand. His stomach clenched as he took a sharp, small intake of breath. It was less than what he had anticipated. His shoulders slumped. Why? The brutality was on another level compared to Georgia's event and should have commanded more. Did his audience prefer white women or were the big spenders not online? Regardless, he'd earnt over a hundred grand in the space of a few days.

HE SAT DOWN and checked his IP connection and VPN before making a few updates to reroute his signal again. This time his IP appeared in Tunisia. *Perfect.*

IT WOULD SOON BE time to find Louisa a few new companions, though he knew it would be a risk. Having viewed the police reports and ongoing investigation, he knew it would be challenging, but he couldn't suppress the burning desire to fulfil the depravity that flowed through his veins. He recognised that everything he did was wrong and that he would eventually face consequences, but the lure of it was intoxicating, and after trying it once, he'd become hooked. The lucrative business had begun when he'd watched snuff movies in the eighties. Very few were real, but they'd ignited his interest and curiosity. From there, it had become an obsession that had led to darker videos and live streams shared with a community of like-minded men and women on every continent across the globe.

For so long, he had been nothing more than a faceless observer until the desire for more had led him to this moment... a killer.

32

KAREN ARRIVED at the station and headed straight for her office. She dropped her bag under her desk, hung up her coat on the back of the door, and made her way to the kitchen in need of a strong coffee to kick-start her day. Jade was already there, lost in her own world, stirring a spoon round in a mug.

Karen appeared in the doorway. "I'll have a coffee, please."

Jade's spoon chinked against the side of the mug as she jumped. She placed a hand against her chest. "Blimey, you frightened me."

"Ha, serves you right for time-wasting." Karen opened a cupboard in front of her and grabbed a mug. There was something about Jade that appeared off. She wasn't her usual chatty self and more subdued than usual. "Everything okay?"

"I guess. I didn't sleep too well. The image of Steve lying in a bed hanging on for dear life stayed with me." Jade rested her hands on the work surface. "What if he doesn't pull through?"

Karen placed a hand on Jade's shoulder. "We need to stay positive. I'm hoping he does. And when he does, he'll need all of us to support him on his road to recovery. And the minute he is off life support and holding his own, then we'll head back down to London to see him again. Okay?"

Jade nodded, but Karen sensed very little optimism behind the gesture. "The best thing you can do is stop thinking about it and keep your mind occupied. Brad will call us if there's any further updates, and until he does, we assume that Steve is stable, and he needs time for his body to heal."

Jade shrugged. "I guess you're right." She followed Karen back to her office and sank into the visitor's seat while Karen went round to her side of the desk and switched on her computer.

Karen sipped her coffee and welcomed the hot liquid as it warmed her belly. "What have we got for updates? I think the clock is about to run out for Louisa."

Jade cradled the mug in her hands. "The team has begun the process of identifying disused commercial or agricultural buildings in relation to where they discovered both Georgia and Raveena. I've asked them to focus on an area halfway between both locations. We found Georgia and Raveena twelve miles apart, so they started working on the area around Farlington and are expanding their search outward."

That made sense in Karen's mind. Perhaps their killer had a base in between and could travel in either direction.

"We're dealing with such a vast area that many of these buildings wouldn't be visible from the road, so we are using Google Maps and Google Images to shortlist locations."

Karen understood the complex nature of the investigation. A radius of six to ten miles round Farlington was an enormous area to search, and she wasn't even sure if they were looking in the right place. "Anything else?"

"Yes. We have identified the tyre moulds taken from Yearsley Woods as Goodyear Vector 4Seasons Gen-3. A common tread. There were certain scores and marks through wear and tear. It's a matter of us matching it up to any vehicles that we come across as part of our investigation."

Preet appeared in the doorway. "Sorry, am I disturbing anything?"

Karen waved her in. "No, of course not. We were discussing Jade's constipation and the fact she's not been for a number two for four days. I'm a bit worried that *things* are backing up now... if you know what I mean?"

"Karen!" Jade shouted in horror as she glared at Karen.

Preet looked from Karen to Jade, unsure what to say or to believe, and offered a weak and awkward smile.

Karen waved off Preet's awkwardness. "Don't worry about it. If you hear deafening and unpleasant noises coming from the ladies' loo in the next day or so, you'll know Jade found relief." Before Jade could interrupt, Karen continued. "Anyway, what can I do for you?"

"I've been looking into the white van seen close to Raveena's car. It's more than likely a Mercedes Sprinter van. The DVLA confirmed there are eight hundred and sixty-seven white vans nationally with a registration plate starting with FP09. They are sending over a list of any registered within the Yorkshire area. I'll work through them as soon as they come through in the next hour."

"Okay, that's great."

"SOCO has taken tyre track moulds from the location, and they also identified a small patch of oil on the floor. Officers from our team visited the area and said it was very remote. There's nothing round there, so it's unlikely to yield any witnesses unless they were passing."

"Bollocks. Okay, Preet. Thanks for that."

"Prunes," Preet said.

"Sorry?" Karen replied.

Preet's eyes lit up as she looked at Jade. "Prunes will get you moving again."

Neither replied to Preet, but Karen nodded in Jade's direction as if to suggest, "there you go".

Preet returned to her desk, leaving Karen and Jade alone again.

"It was a long shot," Jade remarked.

"What? The prunes?"

"No! On the witness front. But we have a partial plate now. That's a good starting point. I'll speak to the press office and ask them to put out an appeal for any sightings of a white van in the area with a registration plate beginning with FP09."

Karen thought about the sighting and its importance as she rocked back and forth in her chair. "What we need to find out is where did Raveena's car go from this location? If this van is connected with the abduction of all three women, did someone help the killer? Did an accomplice take Raveena's car?"

"It sounds like the most plausible option," Jade said. "The three women were somehow forced into the van, and someone drove them away, leaving an accomplice to remove the car and either follow or dump it."

Karen was about to say something when her internal phone rang. She answered it and listened in silence. "Okay, thanks for that. We'll make our way there now." Karen hung up and jumped up from her seat, grabbing her car keys and mobile phone.

Jade sat forward on the edge of her seat, poised to do the same. "What is it?" A hint of concern in her tone.

"The control room took a call from Tim Price, the forest ranger. He's been called to the appearance of an oil slick at Lower Fish Ponds, with tyre tracks leading into the water." Karen leant over her desk and pulled up Google Maps on her computer to check its location. "That's a mile from where Georgia was found. I'll tell the super while you update the team, and we'll meet at my car in ten."

33

KAREN FOLLOWED Jade's directions as they headed north past Yearsley Woods. A dense green curtain of trees and wild hedges blinded their view on either side of the road as they snaked through the narrow and twisty lanes.

"How close are we?" Karen kept her eyes glued to the road ahead.

"Not far. Unfortunately, we'll need to take a right on to an unmade track which will lead us to the pond."

The further they ventured through the landscape; the more certain Karen felt the killer was local to the area. Karen made a big assumption that the oil slick was linked to Raveena's Astra, but the remoteness of the location suggested that whoever dumped something in the pond didn't intend for it to be found for a long time.

"Slow down. There." Jade pointed to a small opening in the hedge on the right.

"Seriously?"

"Yep. Straight down there."

Karen indicated and then wondered why she had

bothered on an empty road in the middle of nowhere. The directions took them from a smooth twisting road to a bumpy and muddy track that tossed them from side to side. She put down the fact that the track was well worn and mostly recent to the presence of other police vehicles at the location already. It was a further ten minutes before Karen spotted the white vans of forensic services through the trees. As Karen pulled up, she saw the track ahead of them snaking off into the distance and appearing to follow the shape of the pond.

"Time for wellies." Karen opened her car door and placed her feet in squelchy mud. "Gross."

Booted up, Karen headed towards the officers gathering on the bank beside the lake. She spotted the figure of Tim Price, the forest ranger, stood among a huddle playing with his beard as he listened to the conversations. He spotted Karen and stepped away from them to meet her midway.

"Detective Chief Inspector. I didn't expect to see you again so soon."

"Me neither."

"Normally I wouldn't bother your lot, but with what's happened recently, I thought I'd call it in."

"I appreciate it. It's difficult to find." Karen scanned the area. Other than the pond, there was nothing but trees and dense undergrowth. She imagined it to be a lovely setting on a summer's day, with the stillness of the water broken by the ripples left in the wake of a few passing ducks.

"You'd be right there." Price stuffed his hands in his jacket. "It's popular for fishing for the few who know it's here. They park at the top end of the track and lug their kit to this spot. Some stay overnight and prefer night fishing."

Karen nodded. "How often do rangers check the area?"

Price shrugged. "Rarely. Couple of times a year as there's a programme of tree preservation and management."

"How did you find out about this?" Karen took a few steps forward and nodded at the shiny black slick that bobbed round in the water close to the edge.

"Ranger on a horse doing his rounds."

"Any idea what's under the water?"

Price tutted and shook his head. "Other than a car, no. Whoever dumped it there knew the area well as they came up the track and took it into the water. I'm not sure if there's anyone in..." His voice trailed off.

"Well, there are too many footprints to pick up any impressions." Karen turned to Jade. "Can you call the underwater search and marine unit? We need divers down there to see if we have a body."

Jade pulled out her radio from the inside of her coat and called it through.

It took an hour for the dive unit to arrive, and in that time, Karen and Jade sat in Karen's car with the blowers on full to stay warm. Price had stayed by the pond to oversee the comings and goings of everyone. One of two vans belonging to the dive unit had hit difficulties as their tyres got stuck in the mud, so Price had towed them out. An hour later, Karen rejoined the officers by the bank as the diver finally finished kitting up, checked the airlines and comms feeds, and got ready to go in.

Tension bristled in the air and uncertainty filled Karen's mind. If this was Raveena's car, then it was another piece of the jigsaw, and one she needed. An uncomfortable ball of worry tickled her stomach as she stomped her feet on the spot and blew out plumes of hot breath.

"Do you feel as sick as I do?" Karen said to Jade beside her.

"Yep."

A diver dropped into the water and took a few moments to confirm the comms were up and the airlines were clear before he gave the thumbs up and sunk into the murky depths. Just a stream of air bubbles breaking on the surface confirmed his presence beneath the water.

"Come on. Come on," Karen muttered under her breath while she listened to the commentary from the diver as he dropped to the bottom of the pond.

Other members of the dive unit remained by the edge, checking the lines weren't getting snagged round submerged branches or weeds.

"That's a negative. I repeat negative. No occupants in the car," came the voice of the diver.

Karen let out a sigh and dropped her head in disappointment.

"Any signs of a body close by?" a dive member asked over the radio.

"Not that I can see. Visibility is poor. I'll shuffle round and have a look."

"What colour is the car?" Karen asked the officer on land.

The diver took a few moments. "White. Ford Focus."

"Not our car then," Jade said.

The ground team relayed the registration plate details and confirmed that the car was reported stolen a week ago and used in a series of robberies on commercial premises.

"False alarm," Price commented, coming over to Karen.

"Afraid so. Thanks for calling it in."

"No problem, DCI."

Karen thanked the dive team and SOCO before heading back to her car. She'd leave the discovery for the robbery unit, and they would arrange the recovery of the vehicle for forensic investigation.

34

Karen walked heavy-footed into the SCU, followed by Jade, who dropped her bag on the floor beside her desk. Their optimism had gone as the team looked on.

"You okay, Karen?" Ned asked. Though Ned had been on the team a while, he always sounded uncomfortable.

"Yeah, I'm okay. I thought we had a potential lead there."

"We all did, and we need a break at the moment," Claire chipped in from her desk.

"We need cheering up." Karen stopped by Jade's desk and leant into her and whispered, "Can you do me a favour and order a few KFC family buckets for lunch? That should cheer everyone up. Let me know how much it is, and I'll send you the money. I'm going to phone Brad for an update."

"Sure, let me know what he says."

Karen pulled out her phone and dialled Brad's number as she walked to her office and shut the door behind her. She stood by her window looking at the grey bleakness outside and longed for the warm spring days to arrive when she could walk round on the grass bare foot again beneath her window and enjoy the dappled shade from the trees.

"Hi, Brad. Hope you're doing okay?"

"Hi, Karen. I'm doing good, thanks. Trying to keep busy, and work is hectic."

"I'm sure. Any updates on Steve?" She fell silent and noticed the heavy sigh coming from the other end.

"No. Stable. That's all they tell us. It's a waiting game. He's due in for surgery, but they're holding off until they're sure his body can cope with it."

"Okay, keep me updated. You lot hang in there. I'm thinking of you all."

"I will. Take care."

Karen hung up and tapped her phone on her desk before pulling up another number. She waited for it to connect. "Wainwright, hello there."

Wainwright cleared his throat. "Ah, Karen. Delightful to hear from you. You've been a stranger MIA."

"Yeah, sorry about that. We've been busy. I came to London a few days ago on a lightning visit to see Steve Nugent in hospital, but I had to head back, boss's orders."

"Yes, I heard about Steve. Terrible news. How is he?"

Karen gave Wainwright a brief update. As the conversation continued, it brought back the nostalgic feeling of old times between them.

"I'm sorry again for not popping in. I would have liked to have seen you."

"Likewise, Karen. I've always got my biscuit box well stocked in readiness, though I must admit, most are probably out of date now."

Karen laughed as they chatted for half an hour. She missed Wainwright. He was bright, super intelligent, and a brilliant listener. He had a knack for making her visits far more bearable. Though he rarely showed it, she'd seen moments where he showed his softer and caring side, which she found adorable. Beneath his cold and hard exterior lay a gentle man.

Jade appeared in the corridor outside Karen's office gesturing with an eating motion through the glass panel.

Karen nodded. "I have to go now, but you take care of yourself. I might be back in London to see Steve again soon. I promise I'll give you a heads-up. You can restock your biscuit box in readiness."

Wainright laughed as he said goodbye.

"Right gang, lunch is on me," Karen shouted, returning to the SCU main floor. "Gather round and grab a bite to eat before Dan nicks it all."

The scene resembled feeding time at the zoo with chairs being kicked back, voices growing louder, and hands reaching for chips, breaded chicken fillets, and corn on the cob. The warm smell of fried chicken filled the air. Karen's stomach rumbled in response as she grabbed a few wings and stepped back into the crowd as everyone hovered round in a circle.

Karen wiped the sauce from her lips and squeezed between the crowd. "Listen, thank you everyone for all your hard work so far. I understand that this case is taking a toll on us, and our progress is slow, but that is the nature of a complex investigation sometimes. A case can go on for days, weeks, even months, without a break and then bam, something pops up, and the result follows. We have Raveena's post-mortem in an hour and I'm praying Izzy comes up trumps for us."

Officers nodded in agreement as they filled their faces.

Karen continued. "We can do this; I know we can. I know time isn't on our side and we can only hope that we're not too late for Louisa. She is relying on us, just like her family. Regardless of how terrible it may seem, or how discouraged we become, we persevere, and we persist until we locate her. Agree?" Karen studied the faces round her. Each one of them had a look of determination as their faces took on an air of seriousness.

"Can I have the last few chicken breast fillets?" Dan asked, breaking the silence round the room.

Officers groaned and laughed as they ribbed Dan and filtered back to their desks with a sense of urgency.

Karen smiled. *Perfect*, she thought as she watched her team with admiration.

35

A CHILL CREPT into Karen's bones as she stood in the examination room. The cold draft from the air circulation system whipped round her face as she wrapped her arms across her stomach and sucked in the cold air.

"Would you like me to turn up the heating? I wouldn't want you to freeze to death," Izzy chortled as she looked up from examining Raveena's body.

Karen laughed at Izzy's black sense of humour.

The post-mortem was already underway by the time Jade and Karen arrived. Karen had sent two of her officers to be there for the start of the post-mortem, and they'd been relieved in all senses of the word when she'd arrived. In fact, they hadn't been able to leave the room quickly enough, with one officer looking green round the gills. Many officers dreaded attending a post-mortem. A combination of the sights, smells, and morbid atmosphere left many trying to hold down their food.

Izzy opened up Raveena's body with the familiar Y-shaped dissection across the torso. When conducting a post-mortem on a female, the medical examiner looped the cut round and beneath the breasts. The medical team removed her organs, conducting weight and measurement readings before the examination.

"What do we have?" Karen cast her eye up and down Raveena's body. Though her skin was milky brown, it was pale and washed out. Karen noticed bruising and deep lacerations around Raveena's ankles and wrists, indicating that she had been restrained. She noted more trauma and bruising on her inner thighs and around her face.

Izzy blew out her cheeks, which puffed up her face mask. She took a step back and cast her eye up and down the cadaver. "Similar injuries and MO to Georgia. Cause of death was blood loss from a deep incision to her inner thigh. However, I would say that this attack was more savage."

"And the sexual assault?"

Izzy rolled her head from side to side to ease the stiffness in her neck. "A bad one unfortunately. She has extensive tears and bruising to her vaginal cavity, but not because of penetration by a penis. I would say a foreign object." Izzy stepped away from the table and returned with a small metal dish. "I recovered this from inside her."

Karen and Jade stepped forward and leant over to examine the evidence. It appeared to be a small, jagged piece of black plastic no bigger than half a thumbnail. Karen's brow furrowed with curiosity. "What's that?"

"A small piece of hard black rubber. If you look at it closely," Izzy said, pointing to one edge, "there appears to be half of a hole punched into the rubber. I can't be certain until it's examined further, but I would say that it forms part of a rubber handle."

Karen sighed. Izzy didn't need to explain further as a picture formed in Karen's mind.

Izzy continued with her assessment. "The victim's

stomach was empty. I would suggest based on examining the digestive tract, that she hadn't eaten for several days."

"Starved?" Jade suggested.

"Possible." Izzy moved round the table towards the head, to where a section of hair had been shaved away by her technician. "She's also experienced blunt force trauma to the skull. There is a deep depression in her skull and large fracture. I also recovered several blades of grass from within the dura mater and arachnoid layers. They are two of the three layers of tissue that sit between the skull and brain."

"That suggests a heavy blow?" Karen looked across to Jade, who took notes.

"I'm afraid so. It's a very particular indentation, so something angular."

"The grass strands may have originated from the location where her body was found."

Izzy didn't agree with Karen's assessment. "Unlikely. The blades of grass were deeply embedded. In my view, the injury and the deposit of grass occurred before she was dumped. We have evidence of blood clotting round the wound, which would suggest she was still alive."

Karen nodded in agreement. "That makes sense. Forensics didn't find any blood deposits round her body or close to the scene."

"Exactly," Izzy replied. "We've taken close-up shots of the injury, and we'll liaise with forensics to see if we can confirm the weapon used."

"Any other injuries?" Jade asked, a pen poised above her notepad.

"You've already seen the deep bruising and lacerations to her wrists and ankles from being restrained. There are bruises to her lower back, grazes to her elbows, palms, and heels, in line with being dragged across a hard surface. We've taken scrapings from those wounds. I noted grit in them and some traces of grease. I would be surprised if they don't come back as a match for the ones identified on Georgia's body."

Karen thanked Izzy for her time before leaving and grabbed a coffee from the café close to reception as they headed back to Jade's car. Once inside, they sat in silence for a few minutes, sipping on their hot drinks, both reflecting on the evidence from the post-mortem.

"He's getting more violent." Jade stared over her cup and through the windscreen.

"I know. Can you imagine the state Louisa must be in if she saw or heard her two friends being tortured and murdered?"

Jade didn't reply, but nodded before she sighed and started her car.

36

KAREN LEFT Jade to update the team on the outcome of Raveena's post-mortem while she put in a call to Owen in Swansea. Tiredness clouded her mind and the start of a headache gnawed away at her. She grabbed her trusted box of Nurofen from her desk drawer and washed down two tablets with a swig of water.

The ring of her mobile distracted her. She pulled a face of surprise when she noticed the caller.

"Owen, I've returned from Raveena's PM and was about to call you."

"Good timing then," he replied. "I thought I'd give you a quick call to tell you we found Karim and have him in for an interview."

Karen sat up in her seat. "Is he giving much away?"

"Not at the moment. Most of our questions receive the usual reply of 'no comment'. We did find him in possession of three phones. Two burners, and one belongs to him. We've downloaded the data from all three phones and are running cell site analysis on them now."

It was another step in the right direction as far as

Karen was concerned. It was slow progress, but she had a gut feeling they were closing in.

Owen continued. "We did get him to open up a bit. Karim was adamant that he had nothing to do with Georgia's death. He admitted to following her several times, but he hasn't seen her in months and hasn't had any contact with her. However, that seems at odds with the data we've pulled off his phone. He messaged her thirty-four times in the last two months, and Georgia only replied to three messages and in all three, she stated that she wanted Karim to leave her alone."

"Unless we can place him in the area, it's unlikely that Karim is our number-one suspect. And I can't imagine that he has turned his hand from dealing drugs to the torture and murder of his ex-girlfriend, one of her friends, and imprisoning a third."

"I agree. Nevertheless, the press is all over Swansea police at the moment, so we need to be thorough even if it's only for elimination purposes."

Karen spent time updating Owen on the results from Raveena's post-mortem. She sensed he shared her shock at the escalation of violence and brutality. They were both of the opinion that it would only get worse if they didn't find the killer soon. Pulling the most important points from the forensic report, she also updated Owen on the detailed analysis of the pollen spores and how they were focusing their efforts on searching disused agricultural buildings.

Having said everything she needed to say, the two of them fell silent.

"You are getting as much flak as me. How are you holding up, Karen?"

"I've had a lot worse. Having done my time in the Met, you become thick-skinned. My focus is on finding

Louisa... hopefully alive. But I know I've only got a few days on my side. He has only just discarded Raveena's body, so my guess is that he isn't going to murder Louisa within the next twenty-four to forty-eight hours, unless something spooks him." Karen rubbed her throbbing temples and considered popping another two Nurofen. "Our latest press appeal asked residents close to abandoned agricultural buildings to alert us if they see any suspicious activity close by. We need them to be our eyes and ears."

Karen was about to continue when Belinda rushed through her office door, a mixture of excitement and concern etched on her features. "Hold on a sec, Owen, one of my team has popped in. What is it, Bel?"

"A local unit has found Raveena's car. Jade has dispatched a few of our team to the location and alerted SOCO."

"Whereabouts?"

"On rough ground beside a lay-by four miles from the woods. Not easily spotted from the road. Because of its location, Jade has instructed for the car to be wrapped in tarpaulin and put on a low-loader before being recovered to the forensic unit to preserve as much evidence as possible."

"Did you hear that, Owen?" Karen brought the phone back to her ear.

"I did. I'll let you crack on with it but give me a shout as soon as you find anything."

"I will do. Speak soon." Karen cut the call.

AN HOUR LATER, Karen made her way to the forensic bay, where Raveena's black Astra was lit up by four arc lights positioned at each corner of the vehicle. A crime scene investigator picked through items that remained in the vehicle, while another photographed and documented them. Karen kept her distance but looked on with irritation. SOCO had a job to do, but in her mind the clock was ticking. She paced round, stopping to examine the outside of the vehicle. A layer of dust and forest debris covered it. The question that played on her mind was whether Raveena had stopped at that spot or if the killer or an accomplice had dumped it there.

Bit by bit, the evidence of their lives was laid out on the floor behind the vehicle. Water bottles, sweet wrappers, a scarf, gloves, as well as spare clothes were found in the boot. The investigator remarked on the presence of hair and clothing fibres across all five seats. She expected most of them to have come from the three women, but she hoped the evidence would point to who else had been in the car. They would take swabs from the steering wheel, door handle, gearstick, radio, and seat belt buckles. All prime locations for DNA from sweat on fingers or saliva.

She left the investigators to it as she rushed back to her team to give them an update. The priority now would be to have all of that evidence collected, documented, and fast-tracked for analysis overnight.

For the first time in a few days, a spark of hope filled Karen with excitement that they were making progress.

37

With Jade and Bel covering the late shift, Karen left the office and headed into town to meet Zac and Summer. Though there was so much to do in the office and a growing list of emails to work through, Karen refused to let Summer down again. She'd been through a lot for someone so young, and this was about helping Summer to regain her confidence about being out in public. Besides, Karen was a phone call away if the case took a dramatic turn.

Karen opened the door to the Happy Valley Chinese restaurant. The familiar spicy and sweet aromas of Chinese food assaulted her nostrils. Her stomach growled in anticipation. There was something about the smell of Chinese food that always evoked such a strong urge to eat everything on the menu. She spotted Zac and Summer further into the restaurant and swerved her way through the tables before joining them. They were both munching on prawn crackers as she arrived.

"I hope you haven't eaten the whole bowl?" Karen

stared at the last few broken pieces of crackers languishing at the bottom.

Zac and Summer exchanged looks of guilt before smiling back at Karen gleefully. "We haven't just been eating prawn crackers. We've been trying to master the art of using chopsticks." Zac fumbled with his chopsticks and tried to pick up his napkin but failed.

"I thought you weren't coming." Summer looked at Karen. Relief washed over her as she sat forward on her chair and rested her elbows on the table.

"And miss out on a free Chinese meal because your dad is paying? No chance!"

Zac raised his brow at Karen. "Who said anything about me paying?"

"Executive decision made by the women in your life." Karen winked in Summer's direction.

Karen gave Summer a peck on the cheek and did the same with Zac. "I don't know about you two, but I'm famished."

The three of them spent the next few minutes going through the menu before placing their order. It wasn't long before a sumptuous banquet of sizzling food arrived at their table. Spring rolls, special fried rice, prawn chow mein, and sizzling beef in black bean sauce. The dishes kept coming. The three of them looked at each other and burst out laughing as a server struggled to find spare space on the table.

"I think we ordered too much," Zac said as his eyes danced from one dish to another. "But they smell so bloody good."

"It looks like a lot, but I don't know about you, but I get stuffed eating Chinese food, and then an hour or two later, I'm hungry again," Karen said.

"Same here. Weird," he replied.

"I didn't think he liked Chinese that much, Summer?"

"It's okay. I have to be in the mood for it. I thought we would try something different rather than pizza or burgers, and Dad told me you love Chinese food so I thought it would make you happy too."

Karen's heart felt like it was about to burst. It was a grown-up and mature thing for Summer to say. She wanted to grab Summer's cheeks and give them a hard squeeze, but doubted Summer would appreciate it in a packed restaurant. Karen had noticed a change in Summer, and it wasn't merely because of what had happened at the hands of the Harmans' associates. There was a slow change in Summer's attitude to life and she had surprised Karen on more than a few occasions with her maturity.

They dived into the bowls and the first mouthful of beef in black bean sauce sent Karen's taste buds wild. She couldn't shovel the food in quick enough. Everything about the evening was perfect. The atmosphere in the restaurant was buzzy, the servers were brilliant, Summer kept winding her dad up, and Karen felt contented. She was on her second bottle of beer, and they were going down quicker than she expected as she listened to Summer beg Zac for tickets to see Usher in concert.

Karen noticed Summer would occasionally glance round the restaurant, her eyes quickly scanning the sea of faces. And each time she did that, her entire persona changed. She became more unsure of herself as she shrunk back into her seat and fell silent before lowering her gaze and staring at her food, pushing it round her plate with the chopsticks.

Zac excused himself to visit the bathroom. Karen put the chopsticks down and reached over to Summer's hand to give it a squeeze. "You okay? Are you having a nice time?" It took a few moments for Summer to reply. Karen noticed her swallow hard.

"Yeah. I get nervous when..."

"I know. But look around you. Everyone is happy and smiling, and they're all having a great time. And you, missy, are doing bloody amazing. I'm so proud of you, as is your dad. And I don't want to make you any more pig-headed than you are already, but I've noticed a change in you in recent months. You've grown up and you're turning into a beautiful, funny, and sometimes annoying young lady." Karen smiled.

Summer's eyes watered before she dabbed them with her napkin. "Thank you. I love you. Thank you for coming into our lives. You've been more of a mum to me than Mum has. I know that sounds bad, but she never really had time for me... and still doesn't."

It was Karen's turn to well up. She cleared her throat and blew out her cheeks. "I love you too. And... I love your dad... sometimes."

They both burst into a fit of laughter as they wiped their tears away. Zac gave them a funny look as he returned.

He took his seat. "What have I missed?"

"Oh, Dad, we were talking about the holiday that you're booking for the three of us to Universal Studios in Orlando next summer. We are staying on Universal property to get early entrance into the parks." Summer placed a hand over her mouth as she burst out laughing, which set off Karen, too.

Zac's jaw dropped as he looked at Summer and then to Karen. "Who agreed to this?"

"We did, didn't we, Karen?" Summer chortled.

"I'm afraid so. And frankly, you have no say in the

matter other than providing us with the sixteen digits across the front of your credit card."

Zac glared at Karen and shook his head in disbelief.

"And, Dad, don't look at Karen like that, or you'll be sleeping in the spare bedroom."

The threat set Karen off again as she rocked back in her chair, her laughter drawing the attention from other diners.

"You can go off people very quickly." Zac tutted and laughed with them. He reached for his bottle of beer and drained the last of it. "That's it. We're going home before you fleece me for anything else."

38

THE MEMORIES of last night still tickled Karen as she arrived at the station and made her way to her office. She wasn't sure how they had gone from talking about Summer growing up to telling Zac that he was taking them on holiday. And though they had only been teasing, the three of them had spoken about it non-stop in the car all the way home. Summer had raced up to her bedroom to retrieve her laptop the minute they stepped through the front door.

The excitement on Summer's face was priceless and though Karen knew Zac couldn't afford it, she had spoken to him in the kitchen and they both agreed that if he booked it, she would pay half of the cost.

Karen sipped on her black coffee, hoping the smell would disguise her garlic breath from last night. Her desk phone rang. It was Kelly asking her to come to her office. Karen groaned. She hadn't engaged in work mode yet, and the thought of Kelly grilling her about the case filled her with dread. Karen grabbed her notepad and pen before heading to Kelly's office.

She peered through the glass and saw her boss alone. Karen knocked and waited before Kelly called her in.

"Morning, ma'am."

Kelly's face was stern as she looked up. "Morning, Karen. Come in. Shut the door and take a seat."

Karen did as she was told and rested her pad on her lap. "Do you need an update on the case?"

Kelly nodded. "Yes. But not at the moment. I need to talk to you about another matter."

"Oh?"

Kelly stared at Karen, her features not giving anything away. "Sally Connell."

"Oh, right."

"Bad news, I'm afraid. The NCA have confirmed that Sally Connell is back in the country."

"Shit. Sorry, ma'am."

"Don't worry. I said the same when I heard the news."

Dread washed over Karen as a sinking feeling hit the pit of her stomach. She'd felt safe knowing Sally Connell was out of the country, but hearing she was back left her on edge.

"The NCA haven't been able to confirm her current whereabouts, but they uncovered intelligence to suggest a plot is imminent to spring Terry Connell from prison. There's a strong possibility she is in London."

Karen's eyes widened. *It's an outrageous plot if that's the case.* Karen had helped to bring the Connells down. Officers had shot Terry in the chest as he'd charged at them with a club hammer. Sally's other brother, Steve, had died in a firefight with armed officers.

"What have prison authorities done about this?"

"They moved Terry to Belmarsh as a cat A prisoner. I haven't got all the details, Karen, but from what they've told me so far, Sally Connell slipped out of the UK. To begin with she was being protected by former UK associates hiding out in the Sierra Nevada hills of the Andalusia region." Kelly tapped a pen on her desk as she clenched her jaw. "However, other intelligence gathered by the NCA suggests she's been in Morocco and Germany, and according to Europol, more recently met up with a Russian OCG in Frankfurt."

"Frankfurt?" Karen blurted out, the development troubling her.

Kelly nodded. "Europe is now a playground for Russian OCGs. These Russian mobsters are untouchable. A recent $30 million fraud led to the money being passed through UK banks, and several lower league football clubs in Portugal were used to launder millions of euros. Blood money from contract killings, arms and drug trafficking, extortion, and kidnapping has been used to purchase a significant amount of Spanish real estate."

"What are Russian authorities doing about it?"

Kelly sighed. "As much as they can, but the OCGs have connections that lead right to the top levels of Russian politics. A lot of Russian OCGs are flexing their muscle and looking to move into the UK. They are already here, but they are looking to take a larger slice of the market. Deutsche Bank last year said that $1.5 billion entered Britain each month without being recorded by official statistics, and half of that cash came from Russia."

"How does Sally fit into all of this?"

"Her connections. There are still many people loyal to Sally Connell and the NCA believe she's offering her network of associates and connections to the Russians in return for their backing and a slice of the action."

"Shit." Karen closed her eyes and ran a hand through her hair. Her headache was returning.

"I need you to be extra vigilant. We'll do everything we

can from our end to protect you, and as yet, we have no credible intelligence to suggest she is looking to settle a score with you. Everything appears to show that she wants to get her brother."

That didn't mean shit in Karen's eyes. What would happen if she sprung her brother? That would make the woman even more powerful and dangerous.

"I will arrange for a tracking device to be placed in your car and your phone today." Kelly shifted in her chair and sat back. "We'll also need to install a panic button and extra cameras at Zac's house. He won't like it, but it's an important necessity. I'll speak to him?"

"Understood, ma'am. I'll call him."

"Be extra vigilant. Keep an eye out for anything suspicious, someone lurking in the street, or a car following you."

Karen pursed her lips and thought about what had happened the other night. "Actually, ma'am, two days ago I thought I was being followed as I headed home in the evening."

"Really? Why didn't you say anything?" Kelly replied.

"Because it appeared as if the car was following me and I took a few diversions to see if that was the case, and at first it looked that way, but then it turned off and never reappeared again. It could have been coincidence that they were travelling in the same direction as me."

"Description of the car and its occupants?" Kelly asked, her pen poised above her pad.

Karen shrugged. "It was dark, ma'am. It looked like a black saloon when they pulled off, possibly a Mercedes, Audi, or BMW. I couldn't see the number of occupants."

Kelly dropped her pen on the desk and sighed. "Okay. I'll update you about the tracking devices once I got the sign off. For God's sake, keep your wits about you."

Karen rose from her chair. "I will do, ma'am. Thank you."

Karen's heart thumped in her chest as she headed back to her office filled with a mix of dread and panic.

39

KAREN RETURNED TO HER OFFICE, sat down, and rested her elbows on her desk. She stared at the glass panel that separated her office from the corridor. Thoughts rushed through her mind and memories resurfaced. Her battle with the Connells felt like a lifetime ago and one she'd left behind. Sally Connell didn't bother her as much as the intelligence which pointed to her new alliances. It seemed as though Sally Connell had risen into the upper echelons of the criminal world. The global connections would present a significant challenge for any national law enforcement agency. Karen had no choice but to take the threat seriously.

SHE FELT a dropping sensation in her stomach as her chest tingled. And though she wanted to focus on the positives, it was hard to see anything but a violent outcome if their paths crossed again. In the end, Karen's investigation resulted in Sally Connell losing a brother and having another one injured.

. . .

KAREN'S LEGS bounced up and down on her toes as she recalled her conversation with Kelly. With a sigh of resignation, she reached for her phone and called Zac to break the news about the extra security measures.

JUST A FEW MINUTES after she ended her call with Zac. Karen rested her head in her hands, taking a moment to close her tired eyes. A knock on the door cut short her moment of comfort.

CALLUM SUTHERLAND APPEARED in her doorway. "Sorry, Karen, bad time?" Callum pushed his glasses on to the bridge of his nose as he loitered. As a senior crime scene investigator on Bart's team, Karen had worked with him on multiple occasions. He was methodical, serious, but easy-going.

KAREN SHOOK her head and waved him in. She could do with the distraction. The call with Zac had been a little frosty. Though he understood the severity of the situation and the extra precautions that Kelly wanted in place, invading his family's privacy infuriated him. Considering everything that had happened with Summer and the Harmans, he was already touchy about their safety.

CALLUM DROPPED into the seat opposite her. He was a tall, slender man with a long neck. His police issue black polo shirt hung from his frame and looked at least a size too big for him. Callum was an intelligent man. Karen had spoken with him about his life and was surprised to learn that he possessed not just a first in biological sciences from the University of Nottingham, but also an MSc and a PhD. He was qualified enough to be a professor or lecturer in academia but had chosen a career that challenged him in a different way.

"WHAT HAVE YOU GOT FOR ME?"

CALLUM HANDED over a report for Karen's reference. "The blades of grass found embedded in Raveena's skull were of an exact match to those of the fairway."

KAREN FROWNED. "YOU SURE?"

CALLUM NODDED. "Sure as we can be. Blades of grass in one field can differ from the next because of factors such as soil composition, exposure to sunlight, and water availability. They cause or result in variations in colour, height, thickness, and other physical properties."

KAREN FELT PERPLEXED. There was no evidence of an attack having happened on the fairway. She continued to listen to Callum's explanation.

. . .

"WE'VE CHECKED AND DOUBLE-CHECKED. There is also genetic variation to take into account. Like humans, plants and grass have their own genetic make-up, which offers their own distinct characteristics." Callum paused as Karen scanned the report before he continued. "The age and maturity of a blade of grass can also contribute to its differences from others. A young blade of grass may have a different appearance and structure compared to an older one. As each blade grows and develops, their cells undergo changes that can impact their physical characteristics."

KAREN CLOSED her eyes to process the information as Callum confirmed they'd obtained samples from different areas of the fifteenth fairway and the results matched. In fact, to be sure, they'd taken more samples from other fairways close to the fifteenth with the same conclusion.

"OKAY. Thanks, Callum. I'll go through the rest of the report and give you a shout if I need further clarification."

CALLUM NODDED AND SCOOTED OFF.

KAREN SPENT the next few minutes scanning the results. The impressions in Raveena's skull suggested a weapon with a thin, flat edge, and the thin markings on her face reflected that. As yet, they were unable to confirm the type of weapon because they needed to conduct further investigations. Karen questioned whether it was a thin pole, but the evidence pointed to the markings having very clear and distinct edges. *Side of a hammer?* That became possible in her eyes because the small piece of black rubber recovered from the inside of Raveena's vaginal cavity suggested it originated from the rubber grip of a hammer.

SHE EXHALED and shook her head as she moved on to further analysis. The buccal swab taken of Charles the hermit had come back clean and there was no match in the system. There were also no foreign hair, blood, or semen traces on Georgia or Raveena. Karen sat back in her chair. The killer had been methodical, leaving little to no clues behind. There was no evidence of the bodies being washed or prepared prior to disposal. So had the killer worn some kind of Tyvek protective suit like the ones worn by the crime scene investigators?

IF THAT WAS THE CASE, then Karen knew they were dealing with someone who may have killed before and was forensically aware. It would be another line of enquiry for her team.

KAREN CLOSED the file and threw it back on her desk. The case was testing her patience. She knew they were getting closer, but the evidence wasn't there. A quick check on the system confirmed that. A few calls had come in regarding the white van sighting close to where Raveena's car was discovered, but nothing of significance. Reviewing social media and phone accounts for all three women had drawn a blank, as had interviews by local officers at each of the three universities.

"BLOODY NOTHING!" Karen muttered through gritted teeth. Karen rose from her chair and headed for the kitchen to rustle up a coffee. She needed time out.

40

SOMEONE from the team had left a pack of chocolate Hobnobs by the kettle, and knowing what her officers were like, they wouldn't last long, so Karen grabbed one and munched through it as the water boiled. There was so much for her to do. The case was taking up much of her time, but there were PDPs (personal development plans) to review for each officer in her team, and now the requests were coming in thick and fast for Christmas annual leave.

It was scary to think that Christmas was a mere five weeks away, and despite her desire to shift her focus to presents, parties, Christmas Day preparations, and countless other tasks, Karen lacked the time or energy to do so. It would be the same as every year... last-minute panic. There was also the risk that she could be knee-deep in the middle of an investigation as Christmas hit.

Her phone rang on the worktop beside her, Owen's number flashing up on the screen.

"Hi, Owen. Did you get the forensic report I emailed

over to you? I've been through it and wanted to keep you in the loop."

"I did. Thanks. I haven't been through it yet."

Karen sensed an upbeat tone in Owen's voice. "No worries. Give me a shout if there's anything you need to discuss. Any news from your end?"

"There is. The cell site analysis on Karim's phones indicate that he was in York two days prior to Georgia and her friends' disappearance."

Karen stopped stirring her coffee. "You're kidding?"

"I'm not. It places him in York but not near Yearsley Woods. The initial story he gave us about not having seen her in months seems at odds with the data we've pulled off his phone. He was lying. We've interviewed him again with the fresh evidence and he admitted that he came looking for Georgia but couldn't find her and left."

"And you believe him?"

"I'm not sure. He seemed genuine enough, but I still think it's a big step up to go from being a drug dealer and harassing your girlfriend to killing her. Unless it was in a fit of rage."

"Out of interest, was there any connection between him and Raveena?"

Owen paused at the other end while he checked the details. "No. They attended separate schools. He claimed he didn't know her that well other than she was best friends with Georgia and Louisa."

"What are your next steps?"

"Officers are still trawling through his phone history, including anything he's deleted. I think this is too big for him to handle. If he had killed Georgia, where did he keep Raveena before killing her too, and of course what has he done with Louisa? It would mean he had stayed in and around the York area before travelling back to Swansea.

The cell site data doesn't show that. We'll keep digging at our end."

Though the update proved helpful, Karen doubted Karim was their man. Karen thanked Owen before hanging up, feeling a further sense of deflation. She grabbed her coffee and headed back to her office, bumping into Jade along the way.

"Karen, I was about to come looking for you. We've picked up Ring doorbell video of a white van passing on a main road near to the dashcam footage. It looks like a Mercedes Sprinter, but we can't see the registration."

"See if the high-tech unit can enhance the image." Karen continued walking back to her office. Jade followed.

"You okay?"

Karen nodded and placed her mug on her desk before stuffing her hands in her pockets and staring at the ceiling. "Yep, I guess so. Just fed up with the lack of progress. While you're here, I've had a call with Owen in Swansea. They can place Karim in York two days before the women went missing." Karen passed on everything that Owen had told her before she moved on to the prickly subject of Sally Connell and the information received from the NCA.

Jade's eyes widened in shock upon hearing of the plot to free the Connell brother and the connections Sally Connell had nurtured. "It sounds like she's got a bloody army on her side."

Karen folded her arms across her chest. "That worries me. If that is the case, then she is a very dangerous woman. Laura is organising tracking devices for my car, phone, and panic buttons at Zac's."

Jade pulled a face. "She won't be coming after you. It sounds like her priority is to get her brother out."

"I hope so. But it pays to be vigilant. It's pissed Zac off

regardless." Karen was about to recap on the forensic report for Jade when Preet appeared in her doorway holding a yellow Post-it.

"Karen, I've taken a call from Derek Redmond, the York golf club manager. He wants to know if you can pop in and see him."

"Did he say what it was about?"

"No. It sounded urgent."

"Okay. Call him back and tell him I'm on my way. Jade, you might as well come with me, and I can give you an update on the forensic report from Callum. It should be up on the system in the next hour." Karen thanked Preet as she grabbed her keys and handbag, agreeing to meet Jade downstairs in the car park in five minutes after she'd been to the loo.

41

DEREK REDMOND WAS NOWHERE to be seen when Karen and Jade arrived. A member of the bar staff went in search of him and came back to inform Karen that Mr Redmond was on the course inspecting the greens and was on the seventh, and despite being called over the walkie-talkie, Redmond said he was too busy to return to the clubhouse. The staff member fetched a map from the pro shop and returned. He circled the seventh and gave her directions on how to find him.

Cheeky bugger, Karen thought. After she had saved his bacon when club members had turned on him, the least she expected was the favour returned by him returning to the clubhouse. As she and Jade left in search of him, Karen noticed a few ground staff moving tools from a small rusty shipping container in the yard at the rear of the building.

"There's something very relaxing about a golf course, isn't there?" Jade said. She stared off into the distance at the manicured greens and lush fairways that surrounded them. Pockets of gently swaying trees and the occasional water hazard broke up the landscape. "My dad is a keen golfer, though his handicap has never improved in all the years of learning. I used to go round with him on a Sunday afternoon, and we spent more time looking for his ball in the rough than anything else." Jade laughed.

Karen glanced at the map to make sure they were heading in the right direction. "You never fancied playing yourself?"

Jade shrugged. "I played a bit. My dad bought me a junior set and we would go to the driving range and practice putting greens. When I got better, we would go to the local pitch and putt course. All the holes there were par three, and the yardage was short to suit the amateur golfer and families."

Karen raised a brow. It was all double Dutch to her, and she never would have put Jade down as a golfer. "Par three?"

"It's the number of strokes, or in layman's terms, hits, that an expert or professional golfer would take to complete a hole. And by expert or pro, I mean someone who is a scratch golfer or has a zero handicap."

Karen shook her head. "You've lost me."

"I'll explain it to you one day over lunch."

"Um, I'd rather you didn't. I have no interest in golf whatsoever. Scratch golfer makes it sound like they've got an embarrassing rash."

Jade smiled and took it as her cue to shut up and continue their search for Redmond in silence. It took a bit of weaving between trees and fairways and asking golfers darting about on golf buggies. Redmond was walking round on the seventh green, tapping spots with the toe of his shoes and making a note on his clipboard.

He wore the same attire that Karen had seen him in before.

"Mr Redmond," Karen shouted.

Redmond looked up and offered a thin smile before tucking the clipboard under his arm. "Ah, good. You found me." His voice carried an authoritarian deepness that was absent the last time she'd seen him. Back then, he was squealing like a pig that was about to be torn to pieces by a pack of hungry hyenas.

"You wanted to see me. Any reason you couldn't talk to me on the phone?"

"Not really, but I prefer to do these things face to face. Call me old-fashioned, but everything seems to be done by the internet, voicemails, mobile phones, and Zoom this and zoom that. Face-to-face conversations appear to be a dying art these days. Don't you agree?"

Karen glanced at Jade and saw the muscles flex in her jaw as she gave Redmond a glassy stare and frowned.

Karen ignored his question. "You wanted to see me," she repeated.

Taking the hint, Redmond huffed. "One of our club members mentioned something as he left this morning. Vinod, York's very own property mogul, comes in a few times a week as soon as the club opens. Does the front nine only, and then heads off to work. Anyway, I digress."

"Hmm," Karen replied in agreement.

"Vinod said that he was blinded by main beams on the night before your victim was found. A large white van was slowly travelling along Lord's Moor Lane. He thought little of it. Frankly, he was more annoyed by being blinded by the intensity of the beams. It's only when he saw the online appeal for a white van that he became suspicious."

"We'll need his contact details."

"I already have them." Redmond opened up his phone and read out the mobile number.

Jade jotted it down.

Redmond looked round and pulled a face. "There's something else. Bit of an awkward one."

"Go on."

"A friend of mine, Terence Derby, club manager at the Oaks Golf Club. He informed me last night that they had kicked out a member yesterday for inappropriate behaviour. When he mentioned the member's name, it rang a bell as we had removed that member from our club for the same reason."

"Inappropriate behaviour?" Karen asked.

Redmond cleared his throat. "Getting drunk in the club bar and making lewd suggestions to female members. He's not a very nice individual when he's had a few pints. A bit of a sexual pest by all accounts."

"And the member's name?"

"Archie Benton."

"Okay. Thank you for your time. We'll stop by the Oaks on our way back." Karen and Jade made their way back to the car park before setting off to the new address.

KAREN COVERED the short forty-minute journey between the two locations, stopping at a petrol station to grab a sandwich and a drink because they were both starving.

"Fancy," Karen said as she turned off the road and drove through the main entrance with elegant stone walls on either side, ornate black gates, and large signage. It was equally impressive on the other side with rows of trees lining the long driveway leading up to the main club-house. Each tree seemed to have been planted an exact distance apart from the next. *Meticulous attention to detail*, Karen thought.

Terence Derby was waiting for them in the main

reception and greeted both officers with a firm handshake and an introduction. Redmond must have called ahead. Derby was a tall, thin man, again wearing trousers, shirt and tie, and V-neck jumper. He had a kind-looking face with a warm smile.

Jade appeared more fascinated with the trophy cabinet than listening to the manager and wandered over to peer through the glass.

Karen continued regardless. "Mr Derby, we understand you had to remove a member from your club for inappropriate behaviour. Can you tell me what happened?"

"Archie Benton was a newish member. Been with us a few months. Owns a local haulage firm, Benton Haulage, in Pocklington. He was always in the bar chatting to female members regardless of whether or not he had played a round. Yesterday, he'd had far too much to drink and tried to invite two female members to a private party. He was very forceful, and our members didn't appreciate the tone and vulgarity he was using."

"Did you hear any of it?"

Derby nodded. "Only the tail end of it. But it was sexual. He suggested the female members might be interested in," Derby cleared his throat and flushed with embarrassment, "masturbating with toys."

By that time, Jade had rejoined Karen.

"Our lady members were upset, and that's not the behaviour we expect or tolerate here, so we removed him from the club and our membership."

"We'll need to speak to the female members involved. Can we have their names and contact details?" Jade asked.

"Diane Butterworth and Carole King." Derby checked his phone and reeled off their numbers.

Jade made a note of their details and stepped away, heading for the exit.

"That will be all for the moment. Thank you for your time, Mr Derby. By the way, do you have CCTV footage covering the bar area?"

"We do."

"Great. Can you send me the footage from last night's incident?" Karen retrieved her business card from her bag and handed it to Derby. "My email address is on there. If you can do that ASAP." Karen smiled and headed to the exit.

42

KAREN FOUND Benton Haulage twenty minutes from the Oaks Golf Club following Jade's directions on Google Maps and had to weave around the potholes and uneven surface as she accessed the yard off the main road via a single lane track that hadn't been serviced in many years.

A large yard opened up in front of her. Two brick buildings stood to the right, and a large concrete yard occupied most of the site with a few old rusty shipping containers towards the far end. Karen parked up in front of the two main buildings and stepped from the car.

"That's interesting," Karen said as her attention was drawn to a line of white vans parked along the boundary wall. From where they stood, she could see a Renault Kangoo, Ford Transit, Renault Traffic, and a Mercedes Sprinter van.

Jade checked the details on her phone. "The Sprinter doesn't have the same reg we're looking for. And none of the others resemble the details we have."

"That would be too easy," Karen said. She turned and headed for the entrance to the building closest to her and stepped into a large reception area with two desks. One desk was occupied by a middle-aged lady who looked up from her work and welcomed them with a smile.

"Hello there, can I help? I'm Janice Crowley, office manager."

Karen pulled out her warrant card. "I'm Detective Chief Inspector Heath from York police, and this is Detective Sergeant Whiting. We are looking for Archie Benton. Is he round?"

Janice's smile faded as she eyed them both up with suspicion. "Um, yes. He's in the back. Can I ask what it's in connection with?"

"We are making enquiries in the local area and need a quick word with him."

"Right. Okay. Let me see if he's free." Janice hesitated, her movements jittery as she turned and hurried away, disappearing through a door at the back, returning a few moments later. "Archie will be out in a sec. Can I get you tea or coffee?"

Karen and Jade declined the offer. Jade wandered off to the noticeboard to scan the health and safety certificates and driver qualification certificates pinned to it.

Karen whispered as she joined her. "Looks legitimate."

The door towards the rear of the building opened and a tall figure of a man appeared, dipping his head beneath the door frame.

"Hello there, I'm Archie Benton. I understand you want a word with me," he boomed.

Karen and Jade spun round, and both gawked at the size of the man. Karen figured he was over six feet tall and tipped the scales at twenty stones. He was enormous in stature and build and wouldn't look out of place in the second row of a rugby scrum. With an enormous barrel chest, a few extra inches round his waist, and a head the size of a football, he wasn't what Karen had expected.

Karen held up her warrant card again and repeated her introduction. "I wonder if we can have a word with you in private."

Benton looked at them and then over his shoulder at Janice, who looked on with interest as she furrowed her brow.

"Sure, come through to the back." He turned and headed for the door, with Karen and Jade in tow.

Karen scrunched her nose as she entered his office. A strong smell of tobacco lingered in the air and left its mark on the yellow-stained ceiling. The room was functional. Two desks, a computer, a monitor on both, with a couple of chairs pushed back against the wall, and half a dozen large-scale maps pinned to the walls.

Benton went round to his side of the desk and dropped into his chair, the frame creaking under his large frame. He rested his arms on the desk and stared at both officers, a blank expression giving nothing away. "Grab yourself a chair if you want to take a seat."

"No, this won't take long. We understand that the Oaks Golf Club expelled you yesterday for inappropriate behaviour. Can you tell us what happened?"

Benton narrowed his eyes. "Why? Have the women made a complaint against me?"

"What makes you think it's women?"

Benton smiled. "Well?"

"No one has made a complaint. But we received information about a conversation you had with two female members. I wanted your version of the events first."

Benton rolled his eyes and shrugged a shoulder. "It was a bit of harmless fun. Listen, I like a drink. And, when I've had a few, I'm loose with my tongue. I said a few things I shouldn't have said. If they want me to apologise, I'll willingly contact them."

"I don't think they'd appreciate any further contact from you at this point." Karen coughed as the smell of tobacco tickled the back of her throat. She imagined it wouldn't be long before her clothes reeked of fags. "This is the second club you've been removed from. Sounds like you're making a habit of this."

Benton's face took on a note of seriousness as he pursed his lips and glared at Karen. "It's a bit of harmless fun. Most of them are a bunch of old farts and can't take a joke. That's not my problem."

"Mr Benton," Karen said, strolling across to the window and taking a peek before returning her attention to him. "It is a problem if you're making crude and inappropriate sexual comments that offend people. In fact, it can be an arrestable offence."

Benton rolled his eyes. "Seriously? Well, I'm not going anywhere. If you're here to arrest me, then get on with it."

"We are not here to arrest you, Mr Benton. I'm making enquiries. You seem to have a very low opinion of women. Is that how you always talk to them?"

"Detective. I don't need to answer any more of your questions. I'm a busy man. I have a business to run. If you want to take this further then take me in for questioning and I'll call my solicitor."

"No. I think we have all we need for the moment. What type of clients do you have?" Karen asked. She glanced over Benton's shoulder at the map of Yorkshire pinned to the wall behind him.

"All sorts. Mainly deliveries for local businesses. We also do the odd domestic or commercial removals. And probably once a month, we do a run for a small family run business that produce packaging material in

Norfolk, and they need their products delivered round the country. Cardiff, Newcastle, Liverpool, even Glasgow."

"Okay, thanks for that. We won't keep you any longer."

Benton rose from his desk and came round to the officers. He towered over them and cast an intimidating presence. "I'll show you out." He didn't wait for them to answer as he headed for his door.

Karen and Jade followed him, and it gave Karen the opportunity to take a peek in the rooms they passed. One was a grubby kitchen in dire need of refurb. Karen paused when she spotted a set of golf clubs leaning in one corner. "Who do these belong to?" Karen paused in the doorway.

Benton stopped in the middle of the corridor and turned on the spot. "Alan. Alan Murray, one of my drivers. He's not here at the moment. He is a member of York golf club and sometimes takes Clive with him. He's my other driver."

"We'll need their contact details," Karen said.

"Why?"

"We discovered the body of a female on the golf course. As part of our investigation, we are contacting every member of the club."

"Right. Janice can give you those details."

Once outside, Karen looked round the yard again. The vans were still there. But Karen's eyes were drawn to the steel shipping containers. "What's in those?"

Benton hovered at the entrance to the building. "Not much. Just odds and sods. Some old equipment and cancelled deliveries. The customers were supposed to pick them up but change their mind."

"It looks like the same one that I saw at York golf club. It has the same logo."

Benton nodded. "It's a spare I had here. They needed

the extra storage space, so I gave them one. It got it out of my yard, so it was a win-win."

"Mind if I look before we leave?"

"Be my guest. I need to get back to work." With that, Benton turned and returned inside just as Jade was coming out having obtained the contact details for Clive and Alan from Janice.

"He is a charming man, with as much social etiquette as a wet paper bag," Jade remarked.

Karen agreed as they both walked over to the two shipping containers. The doors were open on both. She stepped into the first and noticed how cold it was inside. Round her were old machinery and engine parts, but not much else. Stacked boxes filled with cloth samples occupied the length of the second container. Karen rummaged through the first few boxes. It felt like cotton on her fingers and the kind used to make cheapo print-on-demand T-shirts. The labels said Gildan 64000 and Bella+ which meant nothing to her, but she snapped a photo on her phone.

"Come on, Jade, let's head back to the office and get the team to run a check on Mr Benton, his business, and his vans. He was too blasé and rude for my liking."

"I'll call Diane Butterworth and Carole King while they're doing that," Jade added.

43

BACK IN THE office with a million things to do and a growing list of emails in her inbox, Karen rested her head on the back of her chair and closed her eyes for a few moments. Her thoughts spun like a vortex in her mind, and fatigue was doing its best to drain her body of the last remaining drops of energy she had left in her. The end of the day couldn't come soon enough, and with it being late afternoon, it was already dark and cold outside.

She hated the winter. Everything seemed washed out. It was often wet, dull, and miserable outside. With spring being months away, she knew she was in for a long, hard slog. Maybe she needed a blood test? She always felt more negative and miserable during the autumn and winter months. Perhaps she needed a vitamin D booster. The truth of the matter was that she needed the sun on her face and warmth bathing her skin. She wasn't a sun worshipper or anything like that, but always felt happier when she was in sunnier climes. Maybe it was because she was away from work as well, which always had a habit of knocking the stuffing out of her.

Karen opened her eyes and yawned before sitting upright, stretching her arms above her shoulders to relieve the stiffness in her back. She spent the next hour clearing her emails before taking a break to make a coffee and returning to her desk. It had been a while since she had heard from Brad, so she grabbed her phone and dialled his number.

"Karen. How are you doing?"

"Okay. Bloody tired. Can't wait to go home and bury my head in a bucket of wine. Apart from that, tickety-boo."

"I know the feeling. I'm shooting off in five minutes."

"Although I asked you to call me in case of any changes, I had to call. Sorry. Is there any update on Steve?"

"Yes. I stopped by the hospital on the way to work this morning. He's stable and improving. The doctors are optimistic he'll pull through."

Karen closed her eyes and said a silent prayer. "That's great news. He's a fighter."

"He is. They are scheduling further surgery in the next few days to pin and plate more of his injuries before the bones knit in the wrong way. They think he's strong enough to survive the surgery and the quicker they do it, the better the chance of fewer complications in the long run."

"Poor bloke. He's got a long rehab ahead. It's going to take a year, if not longer, for him to learn to walk again."

"That's if he can walk again, Karen. They won't know until he regains consciousness and assess the extent of nerve and tissue damage."

"Yeah. But I'd like to focus on the positives. He will walk again. I know it."

Brad remained silent for a few moments, and Karen wondered if he shared her optimism.

"Are you and Jade planning to visit him again?"

"Definitely. I think we'll wait until he regains consciousness. Anyway, I'll let you crack on. I don't want to keep you from knocking off. I'll speak to you soon."

Brad thanked her for calling before hanging up.

Jade appeared in Karen's doorway, with her coat on and handbag slung over her shoulder. "I'm shooting off now. Do you need anything before I go?"

Karen shook her head and took a few moments to update Jade on Steve's condition. Hearing the news lit up Jade's face, the relief clear to see.

"Oh, I called Diane Butterworth and Carole King." Jade swapped her bag from one shoulder to the other as she did up the buttons on her coat. "They said Archie was charming at first, but he kept looking at their chests and legs more than their faces. They thought he was a harmless lech. However, he became obnoxious and ruder as he drank more. He suggested a threesome and went as far as saying that he had friends who would love to watch."

"Charming."

Jade nodded. "They moved away from the bar, but Benton continued to hassle them, and it led to one of the bar staff warning him off. It became heated, so the bar staff and the men's club captain removed him from the premises. They called a cab for him and sent him packing."

"Right, let's see what else the team find on him tomorrow."

"I've asked Ed to chase down Vinod on his sighting of a slow-moving white van that glared his vision. He's left a message on Vinod's phone."

"Great. Get yourself off now. I'm not far behind you. Night."

"Night, Karen."

Karen checked the time on her phone as she logged off. She had enough time to go home and still enjoy most of the evening.

THE SECOND KAREN walked through the door, Manky padded up the hallway and wrapped his body round her ankles. He purred loudly and demanded her attention.

"Hello, boy. Did you miss me?" Karen hung her coat up on the newel post and scooped up Manky, burying her face in his deep, warm fur. "Missed you today." She smothered him in kisses as she walked into the kitchen to find Zac at the dining table on his laptop.

"Hey, you." Zac rose from his chair and joined Karen as she placed Manky on the floor. He wrapped his arms round her and gave her a lingering kiss.

Karen felt the heat rise as her skin prickled. She stared at Zac and sensed the longing in his eyes as he squeezed her tighter and pulled her hips closer to him. "Hmm. I needed that. Has anyone told you that you're a fantastic kisser?"

Zac stared at the ceiling and raised a brow as if thinking about it. "I've lost count."

Karen thumped him on the arm. "Cheeky git."

"You hungry?"

"Depends on what you had in mind?" Karen teased.

"Exactly what you had in mind, I guess. Well, how about you have a soak in the bath, and I'll bring you up a large glass of wine for starters?"

Karen's eyes lit up. She turned and padded out; her tiredness soon forgotten and replaced with a different hunger her body craved.

44

I CAN'T KEEP my eyes open. It's just me left and I know my fate. He's taken Georgia and Raveena and left me here. This is torture. There is a thickness in my throat and a tiredness in my body I can't fight. It's becoming harder to keep my eyes open and impossible for me to make it to the bucket for a wee, but nothing would come out even if I tried. There's nothing left inside me other than a mental and physical emptiness. It's unbearable. What did I do to deserve this?

A SOLITARY tear escapes from my eye. I can't even cry now. I'm all cried out. He took that from me while I listened to Georgia and Raveena making the most unimaginable sounds that I never thought humans could make. I've lost my voice from my own screams that I hoped would drown out theirs. But it didn't work. I'm broken and want to die. I want to die before he gets to me and does those same things he did to my friends.

. . .

HE IS TALKING TO PEOPLE. I know he is. But they never talk back.

THERE WAS a strange comfort in hearing his footsteps outside as he paced round the room. At least it seemed as though I wasn't alone. But even that's been taken away from me, and I wonder if he will ever come back. I remember hearing him say that he was going to find more friends to join us, but I don't think that happened.

I FEEL sick and dizzy all the time and my body shivers from the cold. There are times I can't stop my teeth from chattering as I curl my hands into a small ball and tuck them into my chest, hoping I slip into unconsciousness and pass away on my own terms.

WHAT IF HE'S left me here to rot? Perhaps he's changed his mind and got fed up or bored, or even got scared off. Does it mean no one will ever find me? My mind drifts to happier things to distract me from the inevitable. Visions of the sun warming my face, the laughter of people round me, the taste of a pepperoni pizza slice, dancing till my feet hurt, standing in an open field and feeling the grass between my toes. Simple things that I'll never experience again.

MY CHEST ACHES as I cough. Thick, sticky phlegm fills my mouth.

.   .   .

I MOUTH A SIMPLE REQUEST. "Please God, take me now."

45

KAREN ROLLED over and snuggled into Zac, listening to his heartbeat against her. "Morning," she said, her voice dry and croaky.

"Morning, beautiful." Zac threw his arm round her and pulled her in tight.

Karen loved moments like this. Sadly, there weren't enough of them. A combination of their hectic work life, long and exhausting hours tied up on cases, and Summer staying four or five days a week, meant they got little "us" time. Last night they'd chatted while Karen had soaked in the bath, with Zac sat on a chair beside her. They'd spoken about the case and Steve's condition in London.

Zac had also mentioned how Summer had searched for Florida holiday ideas, which they'd both found amusing. The list was endless, and Karen questioned if they'd be able to do so much in fourteen days. High on Summer's list was an airboat ride in the Glades, Universal Studios, Aquatica water park, Magic Kingdom, as many roller coasters as possible, and of course, shopping galore in the factory outlets.

As Karen lay there lost in her thoughts about Summer, her chest tightened. Summer was a beautiful and funny teen, and she felt very protective towards her.

"Fancy a bit more of last night?" Zac whispered.

Karen laughed as she pulled herself away from Zac and sat up. The chill of the morning left goosebumps over her naked flesh. After they'd been sure Summer was asleep, they'd made love for the first time in what felt like weeks. It was raw and passionate and something they'd both needed.

"As much as I'd like to say yes, we both have work." Karen spun her legs round and off the bed. "I'm going to grab a quick shower. You can make me breakfast!"

Twenty minutes later, showered, dressed, and fed, Karen slipped on her coat and patted the pockets searching for her keys. "Aw, phew."

Zac was ready too and shouted up the stairs for Summer to get up or she'd be late for school.

Wrapping her arms round Zac's shoulders, Karen stared at her man with warmth in her eyes. "Hey, thanks for listening last night and for all your support."

Zac kissed her. "We're a team. I love you, and I want to be here for you. Remember, I'm here to listen."

She smiled. "You're amazing, and I'm lucky to have you."

"Yeah, I know."

They laughed as Karen pulled herself away and reached for her handbag. "Right, I'm off. I'll leave you to drag Summer into consciousness. I'll see you tonight. Love you."

Zac walked her to the door and waved her off.

ON THE WAY to the office, Preet called with important information that the late shift had uncovered. The news hurried Karen's drive and once at the station, Karen threw off her coat, dumped her bag, and shot off to find Preet.

"Preet, what have we got?"

Karen pulled up a chair beside Preet, who was munching on her breakfast. Turning in her chair to face Karen, Preet put her toast on a plate beside her and wrapped her long dark hair round her ears.

It didn't matter what time of the day or night it was, Preet always looked stunning and beautiful. With dark brown hair halfway down her back, high cheekbones, a flawless complexion, and deep brown near black eyes, she captured the essence of a Bollywood actress.

"The team started a search on Archie Benton. He's not on the system, but one of his drivers is. Nine years ago, Alan Murray was charged with threatening behaviour and assaulting a female. He received a two-year suspended."

Karen's eyes widened in surprise. "Do we know anything about the female?"

"Claudia Butler, ex-partner. She wouldn't give him access to their young son. Murray attacked her, which resulted in a black eye and bruises round her neck. He has been cautioned twice in the past five years for being drunk and disorderly. Slept it off in the cells on both occasions."

"Right, let's have a word with him."

———

PREET AND KAREN parked up in Benton's yard again. The Renault Kangoo and Ford Transit were missing, but the Renault Traffic and Mercedes Sprinter were still there with the rear doors of the Sprinter open. A man with a trolley loaded boxes into the rear.

From the passenger seat, Preet checked her phone. "That's Alan Murray."

Karen and Preet exited the car and covered the short distance across the yard. Murray was a middle-aged man, slight beer belly, unshaven, with a mullet haircut. His jeans hung loosely off his waist, and each time he bent over to pick up a box, the classic builder's bum appeared.

"I've seen better arses on the back of a cow," Karen whispered.

"Good thing I didn't eat all of my breakfast," Preet replied.

"Alan Murray?" Karen asked.

Murray turned and eyed both women as Karen held up her warrant card and did the introductions. He nodded. "Yeah."

"We are following up on several lines of enquiry about the abduction and death of two women and the disappearance of a third. We are interested in speaking to owners or drivers of white Sprinter vans. Is this the main one you use?"

Murray took a cigarette from a pack of B & H in the chest pocket of his Benton Haulage gilet and lit it. In no hurry to reply he tipped his head back and blew out a plume of smoke. "Yeah, it is. Why?"

"We are following up on a few leads. What routes do you take?"

"Mainly local." Murray flicked small pieces of grit on the ground with the tip of his shoe. "Regular drops in Thirsk, Easingwold, Strensall, and Earswick."

"Remote locations." Karen pointed out. "Easingwold isn't far from Kilburn or Yearsley Woods. Did you see three women close to either location about eight days ago?"

Murray shook his head. "I can't say I did. Is this going to take long? I've got a lot to do today."

Ignoring his question, Karen proceeded to ask him about his movements during the time when Georgia and Raveena were discovered, specifically enquiring about his actions at night.

"I do nothing. I come here to do my job and then go to the pub every night. It's better than sitting on my own at home. Play a bit of darts with two regulars. Have a couple of pints. And go home to bed." Murray folded his arms across his chest and stared at the officers. "I assume you've already checked on the system and are aware of my past. I can't afford to get in any more trouble. I'm lucky if I see my boy once a month. That bitch has told the social a load of bullshit."

Karen let Murray continue his rant.

Murray jabbed a finger in Karen's direction as he growled. "But they wouldn't listen to me when I told them she had a bit of charlie on a Saturday night before going out. No, of course they didn't. The dad is always the wrong 'un. You think I'm going to go near another woman again?"

Karen was about to reply when Murray continued.

"And before you ask, no, I don't drive home from the pub. It's a ten-minute walk for me. Deirdre Norris, the landlady at the Cockerel, can vouch for me."

"Okay, Mr Murray, thanks for your time. We'll leave you to get on with your work."

Preet clipped her seat belt in as Karen drove away from the yard. "What do you think?"

"Doesn't like women. Drives a Sprinter van, albeit with

a different reg. Lives alone, so doesn't have an alibi apart from the pub. He's worth looking at. Can you speak to the landlady to confirm his alibi?"

"Sure."

"Let's stop and get a bite to eat before we head back to the station."

46

THE MAN FOUND it hard finding a few friends for Louisa. He'd noticed increased police activity in the towns and signs along the lanes seeking information. The press appeals had made it harder to move about and he switched vehicles to throw them off the scent. The last thing he needed was to be pulled over. There was too much at stake, and it was easy money.

He didn't think he could do it.

To take a life.

They told him the first would be the hardest.

It was.

He threw up after he'd killed Georgia and drunk himself into oblivion.

But he had a taste for it now. The power. He couldn't describe it. All those years of witnessing others do it from behind the safety of his laptop was certain to have impacted him. The torture and brutal murder of the pregnant woman in Canada. Twin sisters in Thailand. A nineteen-year-old university student in China. In Germany, a twenty-four-year-old shop assistant. He'd witnessed countless women being killed over the past few years from all corners of the world, so he'd done his time in the trenches.

He was worried. Finding anyone proved a struggle. Everyone was extremely jittery, but he had punters eagerly waiting, cash in hand. His income over the last two weeks surpassed that of the previous few years. It was like a drug. And he wanted more.

He'd made a few attempts to chat up women, but they'd always brushed him off. His fault for being a bit too forward. He blamed the alcohol. Even the soft touch wasn't working for him. He saw a mum pushing a buggy laden with a few carrier bags of shopping and offered to help. That backfired. He should've punched her when she told him to go away.

There wasn't any other way now. He'd needed to be more forceful, even though that came with risks, but desperate times called for desperate measures. He started the van and pulled away from the lay-by. He'd search again this evening.

47

"HAM, cheese, and tomato toasted panini twice please, and two cups of tea," Karen said to the middle-aged waitress who took their order and sauntered back to the kitchen. She appeared to be in no hurry to get their food, nor clear the tables from earlier diners.

The café wasn't far from the station and a popular haunt for officers looking for a cheapo brekkie or lunch while on shift. A few uniformed officers occupied a long table at the back and tucked into their cholesterol-busting fry-ups. They'd offered nothing more than a polite nod in Karen's direction as she'd entered.

The smell of fried food lingered in the air. Karen's belly grumbled. She'd only grabbed a coffee and a slice of toast this morning before leaving Zac's, so was famished by the time the food arrived. The ten-minute wait seemed to drag on forever.

"This looks good." Preet eyed her food as she scooped up half of her panini and took a hearty bite. She let out a murmur of satisfaction.

"Have you not been here before?" Karen asked. She took a sip of her tea and then took a bite of her panini.

"No. I normally go to the canteen to get my food or bring some in with me and leave it in the fridge." Preet wiped her mouth with the serviette. "I'm trying to be good ahead of Christmas. Too much overindulgence and I already feel fat as a pig."

Karen smiled. She knew the feeling very well. Every Christmas had been marked by countless nights out with the team on pub crawls or indulgent meals. Her mind drifted back to when she was back in London and her sister was alive. Regardless of whether she was on shift or nursing a hangover, Karen had always attempted to visit her sister in the residential care home every Christmas morning until she'd passed away. She would sit in silence and hold Jane's hand. There wasn't much to say other than tell her about what she was doing at work and her plans to visit Mum and Dad later in the day. Despite her sister's lack of response, Karen had still experienced a sense of connection chatting about everyday topics like two sisters would. Nurse Robyn Allen would always pop in with a mince pie and cup of tea, and together they would sit and talk.

Difficult but happier times, Karen thought as she continued eating. Her uniformed colleagues pushed back their chairs, the grating noise on the floor loud enough to cause other diners to look round. She watched as they shuffled out.

Karen and Preet continued to chat in between mouthfuls. She enjoyed these informal moments as they gave her the chance to find out more about her officers and what they did outside of work, while giving her an opportunity to bond with her team.

"Do you get together as a big family?"

Preet nodded, her deep brown coffee-coloured eyes wide with excitement. "It's manic. Family, cousins, uncles, and aunties. It's one big food fest and piss-up for forty-eight hours. How about you?"

"Mine probably won't be as exciting as yours. I'm not sure if I'll see my mum and dad this year. They prefer to go on cruises over the Christmas period, which is fair enough. But I think it'll be me with Zac and Summer. If my parents are here, then I'd like to invite them because they haven't spent much time with them." Karen's phone buzzed in her handbag, so she put down her cup of tea she'd been cradling between her hands and retrieved her phone to see that it was Bart calling.

"Hi, Bart."

"Are you back at the office soon?"

"Yes. I'm with Preet having a bite to eat. Everything okay?"

"Yes. I thought I'd call you as soon as I got the news."

Karen raised a brow, curious at what Bart had to say.

"We've had a DNA match come back on hair fibres recovered from the driver's seat of Raveena's car. A few strands belong to Alan Murray. I've spoken to Jade, and it seems he's a person of interest?"

"Shit. Yeah. We're on our way back from seeing him, bollocks. I'll head back there now. Thanks, mate. I appreciate it." Karen hung up and tossed her phone in her bag. "We've got to go... Now. I'll fill you in on the way. Call Jade for me and tell her to send backup to Benton Haulage and we'll meet them there. I'll settle up and meet you outside."

Fifteen minutes later, Karen's tyres screeched as she turned into Benton's yard. A blue Octavia and a squad car roared into the yard right after her. She instructed her officers to search the yard and containers for any belongings or evidence relating to the three women.

Karen, Preet, and Ty marched into the office, catching Janice by surprise. She recoiled in her chair, eyes wide in shock, hands splayed on her desk.

"Where is Alan Murray?" Karen demanded.

Janice's voice trembled. "He's... he's out on deliveries."

"Is Mr Benton in his office?"

Janice nodded; her voice trapped in her throat.

Karen marched past Janice's desk as the woman sat dumbstruck and firmly rooted to her chair. Preet and Ty followed.

They hadn't reached Benton's office door when it flung open, and his hulking big figure filled the frame. "What the bloody hell are you doing here again? I've just seen the CCTV footage in the yard. You can't just barge in here and start poking round. You must need a warrant or something." Benton threw his arms up in the air in protest.

"There's been a development in our case, and fresh evidence has come to light. We need to speak with Alan Murray."

"He's out," Benton huffed.

"I don't care. Call him and find out his exact location, but do not say why."

Benton sighed before returning to his desk, with the officers following. He called Alan to check where his next drop was before hanging up and relaying the information to Karen.

"What has he done wrong? Is it about his old lady?"

Karen shook ahead. "As I said, this relates to an ongoing investigation involving the abduction of three women, two of whom have been murdered."

Benton frowned, deep crease lines furrowing his brow.

He stared at the officers as he pursed his lips. "I can't see how Alan would have anything to do with that. Although he has been in trouble before, I believe in giving everyone a second chance to start their life again. I gave him that opportunity. He wouldn't screw up."

"I'm not at liberty to discuss the case with you. We'll catch up with him. I'm leaving one of my officers here." Karen turned and nodded at Ty. "He's going to watch you like a hawk. If you take a piss, he's going with you. Under no circumstances are you to contact Alan Murray. If you do, I will arrest you for interfering with a police investigation. Do I make myself clear?"

Benton glared at Karen, his hands curled into fists, annoyed by her tone.

Karen headed back out to the yard to find her officers checking the parked vans and the shipping containers at the far end. Karen headed over to them. The boxes she had seen on her earlier visit were now spread out on the ground and officers were rooting round deep inside each container.

"Karen," Claire said, "There are rolls of silk fabric tucked away at the back of the container. One of them is dark blue. It seems frayed as if someone has torn off a piece."

Karen stepped into the container and looked for herself before coming back out. "Claire, can you put in a call to get SOCO down here? I want these containers and vans seized and examined."

"Will do." Claire pulled off her latex gloves and retrieved her phone.

Karen and Preet rushed back to her car. They needed to track down Alan Murray.

48

BENTON HAD CONFIRMED Murray's location close to Easingwold. The problem was that was forty-five minutes away. Karen had ordered unmarked cars to the area to locate him but to keep their distance until she arrived.

With sirens blaring through the countryside, Karen followed behind a marked police car as they raced to the location.

"Come on!" Karen hissed as she gripped her steering wheel. They flew through Claxton, West Lilling, and then Stilington. Preet listened on the radio to the running commentary given by officers searching for Murray. "He can't be that hard to find. He's driving a bloody white van," Karen fumed as she thumped her steering wheel. She shook her head and muttered to herself. They were close. Her gut instinct told her that. This was their strongest lead so far, and she wasn't prepared to let it slide.

She approached the outskirts of Easingwold. A small, charming market town dating back to the twelfth century with picturesque streets, a cobbled market square, and historic buildings preserved over the centuries. It offered its few thousand residents a stunning countryside on its doorstep.

The marked vehicle ahead of Karen cut its sirens and lights as it came to a halt on the side of the road opposite Easingwold football club. Karen pulled in behind and waited a few moments for an update from the officers searching the town before deciding what to do next. Four further patrol cars pulled up behind her.

Every officer hated the wait in situations like this. Time seemed to slow, and impatience grew. There was the sense of needing to get on with it. It was a while before news came in that a unit had spotted the white Sprinter van with Murray unloading boxes from the rear. She instructed three of the patrol cars behind her to move off and position themselves at the three main roads out of town in case Murray did a runner, and the fourth to stay here in case he came back this way.

"Let's move off. Silent approach," Karen instructed. The car in front of her sped up with Karen following. Tension gripped Karen's stomach as they closed in from different streets, flooding the area with police vehicles. Her heart hammered in her chest and her mouth ran dry. She tensed upon spotting the Sprinter van fifty yards ahead. "Move in now!" Karen ordered. Within seconds she screeched to a halt at the rear of the van, with other police units boxing the vehicle in.

Murray was in the vehicle's rear pushing a box towards the rear doors. His eyes widened in shock as he saw Karen and the other officers running towards him.

"Get out of the vehicle!" Karen shouted.

Murray did as he was told. He looked shocked and wide-eyed as he took in the scene round him as half a dozen officers crowded the rear of the van. Stumbling and swaying, he clambered out, each of his arms being grabbed by an officer.

As he was led on to the pavement, Murray's voice became strained. "What have I done?"

"Alan Murray, I'm arresting you on suspicion of abducting three women. I believe you may have been involved in the murder of two of them and imprisoning the third." Karen read him the police caution before officers placed him in the rear of a patrol car.

Karen stared into the cargo area of the Sprinter. A dozen brown cardboard boxes sat stacked against one side, held in place by green bungee elastic cords. Karen turned to the officers gathered round her. "Let's get Murray back to the station and can someone organise for the van to be recovered back to forensics."

It was a good stop, in her opinion. No drama or risk to the public. Silent and swift. Their presence had already attracted a small gathering of locals on the pavement, looking on with interest. A small huddle talked in hushed tones. It wasn't a busy road, and traffic was light, so it didn't take them long to clear the scene and allow traffic to flow again.

49

THE DISHEVELLED FIGURE of Alan Murray dressed in a white Tyvek paper suit sat on one side of the interview table with Karen and Preet on the opposite side. Once introductions had been made for the tape, Murray declined the offer of legal representation. He sat with his fingers interlocked on a table, the tips of his fingers on his right hand stained yellow from years of smoking cigarettes. His teeth fared little better with a grubby, yellow matte stain.

"I haven't abducted anyone," Murray said. "Why am I here?"

"Alan, I am the senior investigating officer handling the case of three young women who have gone missing, two of whom have been murdered and the location of the third is unknown."

Murray nodded. "Yeah, I'm aware. It's all over the bloody news. What's that got to do with me?"

"We believe that a white Sprinter van may have been involved in their abduction. And you drive one."

Murray shrugged. "So? It's a common commercial van. I bet there are loads of them round here."

"You're probably right. However, we discovered the vehicle belonging to one of the victims, and a detailed forensic examination revealed hair fibres on the driver's seat. Several of those hair fibres were an exact DNA match for you. How would they have got in that vehicle?"

Murray's eyes widened in disbelief. "I dunno."

"That's not good enough. At what point did you come in contact with them?" Karen probed.

Murray separated his hands and rested them on the table, splaying out his fingers. "I'm telling you, I know nothing about them. I've never met them, and I've never spoken to them. Besides, I've given you an alibi, so you know I'm not the one who did it."

Karen opened up a brown Manila folder and pulled out a witness statement. "Yes. My officers spoke to Deirdre Norris, the landlady at the Cockerel, this morning. She confirmed you are in the pub most nights and were there on the nights in question."

Murray threw his arms up in the air. "Well. There you go. I'm in the clear."

Karen held up a hand to silence him. "Deirdre cannot confirm with any certainty whether she saw you all night on the dates in question." Karen glanced at the statement before continuing. "She said you pop out for a fag every so often and come back to order another pint. But there have been times when you don't return. Where do you go? Do you go looking for women?"

Murray slapped his hand on the table. "You've got to be bloody kidding me."

Karen removed three pictures of the women from her folder and slid them across the table. "If only I was. Did you have anything to do with abducting Georgia Caraway,

Raveena Chowdhury, and Louisa White?" She tapped each photo.

"No!" Murray shouted. "I don't know what you're talking about. I've never seen them."

Despite insisting on his innocence, Karen pushed on. "Alan Murray, did you murder and then dump Georgia Caraway and Raveena Chowdhury?"

Murray's face reddened with rage. His eyes bulged and stood on stalks. "Are you not listening to me, woman?"

"Oh, so you're getting all macho. Is that how you talk to women? Is that the only way you can be a man... in the loosest sense of the word?" Karen replied.

"Just answer the question," Preet interjected.

"No, for the hundredth bloody time."

"Have you any information on the location of Louisa White?" Karen pressed.

Murray rolled his eyes and stared up at the ceiling, before resting his elbows on the table and burying his face in his hands. "No," came back the muffled reply.

Karen ended the interview and returned Murray to his cell twenty minutes later when she'd exhausted the interview and made no progress.

———

"WHAT DO YOU THINK?" Preet asked. She walked alongside Karen as they headed up the stairs to the SCU.

"The usual denial bollocks. We have the DNA link at the moment, but we need more. Murray's alibi is leaky. We need cell site data to determine if he was in the area twenty-four hours before and after Georgia and Raveena were found." Karen pulled out her phone and sent a text to Ty asking him to secure Murray's golf clubs at the yard for Bart's team while they were there.

"What do you want me to do?"

"Preet, can you organise a search of his house? We have his keys and phone, so arrange for the high-tech unit to download the phone logs and GPS data."

———————

AN HOUR LATER, Karen slid the key into the door lock at Murray's address. It was a small terrace property with white, peeling paint on the exterior walls of the house, faded green paint on the door, and a worn cream carpet in the hallway. A stale tobacco smell assaulted her nostrils as she stepped inside the property. It was dark and gloomy. Cream Anaglypta wallpaper lined the walls of every room on the ground floor.

"You two search upstairs," Karen said to the two officers behind her. Preet and Karen moved through the downstairs rooms. It was sparse and lacked personal touches. Newspapers and magazines littered a small dining table in one room. Worn brown leather sofas took up much of the living room, and a small thirty-two-inch TV sat on its own stand in front of the window. Empty beer cans spilled over the small bin tucked between the two armchairs, and a couple of random prints hung from the walls, which did little to brighten up the room.

"The place could do with a proper dusting and hoover," Preet remarked. She stared down at the grubby carpet and spotted a scattering of fag ash.

Karen noted an old Dell laptop resting beneath a cushion. She placed it inside a plastic evidence bag and left it by the door. There was nothing out of the ordinary down here, and no suggestion that the women had been in the property. There was no basement and according to officers who had searched upstairs, the loft was tiny and impossible to stand up in. A small garden with overgrown grass, an old shopping trolley once used as a makeshift BBQ, and a garden bench that had seen better days, offered no further clues. It felt like a fruitless exercise and waste of time.

"There's a row of garages at the end of this terrace," Preet said. "You can see them from the far end of the garden."

Karen wondered if any of them belonged to Murray. A call back to the station confirmed that garage number four came with the property.

Together with the two uniformed officers, Karen and Preet left the house and headed to the garage block. The numbers on the front of the garages had long worn away, so Karen tried the key on Murray's bunch in each lock until she found the one that fitted. The garage was in marked contrast to the house. Cluttered and almost full to the edge. Taped up boxes, an old rusty bike, some weights, photo frames, and even sacks of clothes.

"Christ, we could be here all day!" one officer remarked.

"I'm afraid so. You'd better search then if you want to get back for the end of your shift," Karen remarked as she stifled a laugh. "We'll head back to the station with Murray's laptop. Call me if you find anything."

IN THE TIME they had been gone, the high-tech unit had expedited the search on Murray's phone with interesting results. Karen perched on the end of Preet's desk as she read the report. Murray had signed up to several dating apps, his membership active on all of them. What interested Karen further was his photo gallery which revealed photos of women, often from behind and close-up.

"Creepy," she commented. Karen handed the report to Preet.

"What a weirdo," Preet said. She turned one of the photos from the image gallery a hundred and eighty degrees to see it was taken up the skirt of a woman.

"A fixation with women. Violence towards women. A weak alibi. DNA evidence. It's not looking good for him." Karen slid off Preet's desk and stood up. "All helpful, but it doesn't get us any closer to finding Louisa." Karen headed back to her office. She'd let Murray sweat for an hour or two before she interviewed him again.

50

By mid-afternoon, Karen was in the middle of interviewing Alan Murray again. With a strong black coffee in one hand, Karen flicked through her notes as she fired questions at Murray. Despite her pressure, Murray insisted on his innocence. The case rested on one piece of evidence, his hair fibres in Raveena's car. It wouldn't be enough for the CPS, so she needed more.

It was a fine line, and one Karen had to be careful about crossing knowing that Louisa was still missing. If Murray was responsible for their abductions, then she couldn't let him clam up and refuse to help.

A knock on the interview room door stopped Karen in her tracks. "What now?" she whispered as she suspended the interview and left Preet to watch him while she stepped out. Jade stood in the corridor spinning her lanyard around her finger.

"Sorry to disturb you, Karen. There's been an attempted abduction of a lone twenty-six-year-old female out walking her dog. Not sure if it's connected to our case, but..."

"Shit. Whereabouts?"

"It took place between Strensall and Lilling Green. I thought it might be of interest because Strensall was one area where Murray had a regular drop-off."

Karen paced round the corridor for a moment as she thought it through. "It couldn't have been Murray because he's been with us."

"I know. She didn't see the assailant because he attacked her from behind and tried to drag her backwards, but the dog bit him. The victim said he drove off in a large white van. Her impression was that it bore a resemblance to a Transit van. Officers are bringing her in now to get a full statement. I thought you'd like to speak to her."

Karen nodded. "Maybe there were two of them? Murray has an accomplice?" Karen placed her hand on the door handle and looked at Jade. "I'll wrap up here and then we'll talk to her."

Karen rejoined the interview. Murray looked uninterested as he played with his short, grubby, yellow fingernails. Karen jotted down a few words relating to the attempted abduction and showed Preet, who nodded once.

"Alan, I still have a strong suspicion that you may have been involved in the abduction of three women. I also think an accomplice has helped you. After all, anyone would find it challenging to abduct three women simultaneously unless they were forced at knife or gunpoint. So, who have you been working with?"

Murray sighed and shook his head. "Give me strength. I'm telling you, I had nothing to do with it."

Not wanting to let it go, Karen continued to push. "Who are you working with? Give me a name."

Murray shook his head again.

"For the tape, Alan Murray has shaken his head in response to my question." Karen closed her folder. "Interview terminated." She stated the time and told Preet to take Murray back to his cell.

THIRTY MINUTES LATER, Victoria Endelby sat in the victim suite nursing a hot, sweet tea while she dabbed away the tears. Her body shivered from shock.

Karen and Jade sat in the comfy armchairs opposite her. Karen studied her for a few moments. Victoria had piercing blue eyes and mousy brown hair pulled tight in a ponytail. Sporting a green waxed Barbour jacket, dirty riding jodhpurs, and knee-length boots with dried mud on them, she made quite a statement. With an earthy smell, it was as if she spent most of her day outdoors. She wondered if Victoria worked on a farm.

Having already done the introductions, Karen gave Victoria plenty of time to settle and calm down, exchanging pleasantries to begin with.

"Victoria, can you tell us what happened? Take your time. There's no rush," Karen reassured her.

Victoria put her cup down, her right hand still trembling. She blinked hard as she stared at the ceiling. "After feeding my horses at the stables, I was walking back with Dexter, my dog. While Dexter ran ahead through the tall grass, I had my earbuds in, listening to music. Despite not hearing anything, I remember walking past a white van parked on the side of the road. When I glanced in, it was empty. The next thing I knew I felt a man's hand come round from behind me. He clamped it tight over my mouth and pulled me back. I tried to scream but his grip on my mouth was too tight. His hand felt huge. It covered my mouth and nose. I couldn't breathe." Victoria fell silent for a few moments as her eyes darted about, her mind replaying the scene. "I saw Dexter running back to me. The man let go as Dexter bit him. Gasping for breath, I fell to my hands and knees. I was... in... shock. I couldn't move because I was so scared."

Noticing the swell of panic rise in Victoria as her chest heaved, Karen intervened. "It's okay. Take your time."

A minute or two later, Victoria continued. "My mind was telling me to run, but... but I couldn't move. I couldn't move, as if I were glued to the floor. I heard Dexter growl and the man scream. Then I looked over my shoulder and I saw him running back to the white van with Dexter chasing. He got in and drove off. Dexter gave chase and stopped in the middle of the road before running back to me. If it wasn't for Dexter..."

"Do you recall any of the registration details?" Karen asked.

Victoria shook her head. A look of exasperation on her features as she shrugged. She whispered. "I'm sorry."

Karen smiled. "Hey, there's no need to apologise. You've been through a traumatic experience. Is there anything you remember seeing or hearing about the man? His voice? What he wore? His physical features?"

Victoria shook her head again. "He said nothing. He was white and very strong. Much bigger than me. I heard his screams when Dexter bit his leg." She paused for a moment and narrowed her eyes. "He had rough skin on his hands. I've felt hands similar to that before. I've got friends who owned farms and they always have rough and callous hands from working outdoors. He might have a job in farming or building?"

"Okay, that's helpful. Anything else? What about his height?"

Victoria looked at the floor and after a brief silence, nodded. "I'm five feet six, and he was taller. I can't remember what he wore other than jeans and a grey fleecy thing. Sorry, but I was on my hands and knees. I struggled to focus. But I remember his breath. A strong smell of cigarettes."

Karen handed over her business card. "Thank you for your time, Victoria. I know this has been difficult for you, but it's been helpful. I'll arrange for one of our officers to take you back home."

As Jade showed Victoria out of the suite, so many questions swirled round Karen's mind as she gathered her notes and headed back to the SCU. Murray had an accomplice, and she knew who the likely suspect was. He fitted the description. She needed to prove it.

51

BACK AT THE SCU, Karen stood in front of the whiteboards and stared at the collage of information that covered them. Despite her best efforts, her eyes were drawn to Louisa. A mixture of optimism and dread filled her. Within a short time, someone had murdered Georgia and Raveena and had disposed of their bodies. The team needed to stay hopeful that Louisa was still alive. But Karen thought about the timescales, and if the killer had stuck to his pattern of killing, then Louisa was already dead. If that was the case, it would turn the investigation on its head.

Karen tapped a finger on her chin as her eyes darted round the board. The team kept searching for disused or abandoned farm buildings, and so far had identified and visited over seventy. Kelly had drafted in extra officers from neighbouring forces to assist the search, and now there were more than one hundred officers working on the case. Every snout, recently released prisoner, and street rat were being targeted for information.

This was the largest investigation that Karen had been

involved with, and with the eyes of the senior management watching her every move and demanding regular
updates, she had never felt so much pressure.

Ed came over and stood alongside her. With a mug of
tea in one hand, and his other stuffed in his trouser
pocket, he studied the board with her. "I pray for her
family that she's still alive."

"I'm not a religious person, but I'm praying too. If
we've ever needed a divine miracle, it's now."

Ed nodded. "Mind you, even if we find her, I can't
imagine how she'll ever recover from this ordeal. I can't
even imagine that kind of trauma."

"I know. So much of her life ahead of her, and if she's
lucky enough to survive, she will spend most of it
attending recovery counselling, grief counselling, and
being trapped at home because she will be too scared to
do the things she loves the most."

"Our search for further CCTV or doorbell footage on
the road leading away from the petrol station drew a
blank."

Belinda interrupted the conversation as she joined
them at the front of the room. "Karen, I've spoken with a
CSI who examined the golf clubs Ty confiscated at Benton
Haulage. Under a UV light they've identified small traces
of blood and human tissue."

Karen's jaw dropped as she glanced at Belinda and
then Ed. The three of them stood stunned by the fresh
evidence.

Belinda nodded as she raised a brow. "They've taken
swabs from the clubs. Benton said they were Alan
Murray's set. If that is true, that's further damning
evidence of Murray's potential guilt." Belinda checked her
notes before continuing. "We found blood traces on the
shaft, as well as the head and face of the club." Belinda

checked her notes before continuing. "The CSI confirmed that someone had cleaned the clubs. Probably to remove the evidence, but minute blood and tissue traces were still embedded in the grooves of the club face."

Karen clapped her hands in relief. "That's brilliant news, Bel. We may have found one weapon used to beat Georgia and Raveena to within an inch of their life. Izzy's report on both victims identified a striated pattern of indentations on the side of their faces. I'll bet you a tenner that those indentations line up with the grooves on a club face from that set."

"Murray must be our man," Ed said. "Forensics need to prove that for us. If they can lift his DNA from the rubber grip, and we can find the weapon used to cause the thigh wound in each victim, then we've got him."

Karen agreed. "Anything from Murray's laptop?"

"Nothing yet. Still waiting on the report."

"Speak to the high-tech unit and ask them to hurry up."

The three of them headed back to their desks. The case was gathering momentum, and the prospect of knowing they had a suspect in custody with evidence building up against him meant they were closer to finding Louisa.

Karen logged into the database to review the evidence gathered so far. The fingertip search of Murray's house continued, as did the forensic review of Raveena's car. Information was being added to the case file every few hours. A recent addition by a CSI less than an hour ago piqued her interest. The team had pulled blue fleece fibres from the driver's seat and found a few of Murray's strands of hair attached to them. Karen checked the entry again. Blue synthetic fleecy fibres. She clicked open another file to see if any of the belongings from Georgia,

Raveena, or Louisa matched that. Nothing. Izzy's report on both victims didn't find any blue synthetic fibres on their skin, and only silk ones on Georgia.

Karen put in a call to Bart.

"Karen, how can I help?"

"Bart, have your team discovered any blue fleecy items of clothing at Murray's house?"

"Let me check the cataloguing file. I know they've gone through all his clothes and bagged them for evidence."

It was a few moments before Bart came back to Karen, who waited on the line. "Nothing. They haven't done detailed swipes from his sofa or bedding yet. But he doesn't have blue fleecy clothing."

"Okay. Thanks, Bart." Karen hung up and rose from her desk and made her way down to the custody suite.

Murray threw a cursory look at Karen as she appeared in the doorway of his cell flanked by a custody officer.

"Can we get you anything? Tea, sandwich, water?"

Murray sat on the edge of his bed and stared at the floor. He cast a sad figure as he rested his elbows on his thighs and clasped his hands together. "Can I go?"

"I'm afraid not. We're still examining your house, garage, and belongings."

"I'm telling you, I've done nothing wrong."

"We'll be interviewing you again soon. You'll have your say then." Karen leant on the door frame. "I suggest you seek legal support. It will help."

Murray shrugged.

"Just a quick question. Do you own any fleecy clothing?"

Murray bowed his head, still unwilling to meet her eyes.

"Alan?"

It felt like hours before Murray nodded. "I've got a fleecy Benton Haulage jacket. I leave it at work. Janice wears it sometimes when she's cold in the office. The gaffer is always pinching it. It's become a bit of a running joke I own it, but never see it, let alone wear it. In fact, the gaffer has stretched it. The fat git."

"What colour?"

"Blue. It's one of the old ones. The new ones are grey."

Karen stood in silence, the cogs spinning at warp speed. Her eyes widened and she smiled as everything fell into place and confirmed her suspicions.

Archie Benton.

Karen let the custody officer close the cell door as Karen raced back to her team.

52

KAREN and all available officers piled into pool cars and raced in the darkness towards Benton Haulage. Everything made sense now as she hung on to the grab handle above her seat, the car lurching from side to side as it weaved in and out of the traffic. The blare of sirens caused panicked drivers to swerve out of the way as flashing blue lights bounced off the buildings.

The control room diverted all available patrol cars to the location, which led to more than a dozen police vehicles converging on Benton Haulage.

A sharp right at a set of traffic lights led Karen to bang her head on the B pillar. "Get us there in one piece for Christ's sake, Jade." Jade ignored her as she pulled on to the opposite side of the road to overtake a queue of slow-moving traffic. Police vehicles ahead and behind her did the same.

Everything made sense, and Karen needed to prove it. Her stomach lurched and her heart thumped in her chest as she clenched her free hand into a fist. It had to be

Archie Benton not Alan Murray. Murray was a tactical diversion.

The team soon left the outskirts of the city and hit the pitch-blackness of the countryside as they raced towards Pocklington. Karen gazed out the window at the blanket of darkness enveloping them, with only the headlights from each vehicle illuminating their immediate surroundings. Every scenario flashed through her mind. Would he be there? Would the situation turn violent? Were they too late to save Louisa?

Just moments before leaving the station, Karen had briefed her team following her chat with Murray. She had tied all the elements together, so they had a clearer picture. It was the first time in days she had seen a wave of excitement wash across their faces and an eagerness to jump out of their seats to capture this monster and rescue Louisa.

"Come on! Come on, push!" Jade said through gritted teeth as she nudged the car closer to the one in front. "This isn't fucking toytown."

Karen smirked. "Keep your distance. I don't want to explain to the super why you ended up writing off a pool car."

"Yes, Mother," Jade replied. She eased off the accelerator and gave Karen a disbelieving shake of her head.

The convoy of cars braked as each one took a sharp left through the open gates of Benton Haulage. They fanned out as they came to a halt. The first thing Karen noticed was the absence of the white Transit van she had seen on earlier visits. The officers congregated in a big huddle waiting for Karen's instructions. She ordered a few officers to search the outbuildings. Dread washed over her at the prospect of discovering that Louisa had been mere yards away on their earlier visits.

Karen, Jade, and several other officers headed for the main office where they found Janice behind her desk. She threw herself back into the chair, her hands up in a mixture of surprise and surrender as her jaw dropped. Her lips moved in silence like a goldfish.

"Where's Archie Benton?" Karen demanded.

Janice didn't move, her body rigid with shock.

"Benton! Where is he?"

Janice shook her head as she struggled to form words. "He's... He's... Um... He's not here."

Karen gestured for officers to search the offices at the rear of the building. She took a few steps forward and planted the palms of her hands on Janice's desk and stared at the woman. "Right, so he's not here. If you don't want to spend a night in the cells where my officers will strip-search you and do an internal body cavity examination, I will ask you again nicely. Where is he?"

Turning to Jade and giving her a sly smile, she returned her attention to Janice.

Janice's hands, still raised in surrender, and now trembling, ran her eyes across the officers all staring at her. "I don't know. He took the keys to the Transit and said he needed to check on something. I tried to call him earlier, but he didn't pick up."

"Jade, dispatch units to Benton's house in case he's gone there."

Jade stepped out to make the call as the other officers returned from searching the offices at the rear. Benton wasn't there.

"Janice, where else might he be?"

Janice lowered her hands and rested them on her lap as she took deep breaths to control the panic swelling in her chest. "I don't know. I'm always here till late and Archie always pops out one evening a week and comes back to lock up, but always reappears wearing different clothes to what he left in." Janice furrowed her brow.

"Other than this haulage yard, does he have access to any other commercial or agricultural buildings in the area?" Karen asked.

Janice nodded. "He has another smaller unit close to here. Alongside running a small haulage business, he used to service farm vehicles there. As the haulage business grew, he shut down the servicing arm a few years ago and made the transition to this site. As far as I know, the former site is run-down and derelict now."

Karen turned to her officers, and judging by the look on their faces, knew there were thinking the same as her. "I need that address now, Janice."

Janet scribbled down the address on a piece of paper and handed it to Karen before the officers raced back to their cars.

53

THE DISCOVERY of the secondary site led them to a desolate stretch of abandoned and crumbling structures, a ghostly echo two miles shy of Pocklington. Karen, with a gesture commanding silence, guided the convoy of vehicles. They filed through the entrance, their presence announced only by the sinister whisper of tyres over cracked concrete. To the side, a rusty gate, once a sentinel, now lay useless, ensnared by the relentless grasp of nature.

As Karen and her team emerged from their vehicles, a palpable hush enveloped them, the air thick with anticipation. Hidden from the casual glance of the road by an oppressive canopy of branches, a white Transit van lurked in the shadows, its presence a silent scream in the quiet of the scene.

In that moment, with an eerie certainty that chilled to the bone, they all knew. Archie Benton, the monster they hunted, was woven into the very fabric of this godforsaken place.

Perhaps Louisa was still alive. Perhaps she could be

saved before she met the same brutal fate as the two who came before her.

Karen clung to that hope like a lifeline.

Jade pulled up a satellite image from Google to get a clearer picture of where everything was situated. As far as they could tell, seven buildings of varying sizes were spread out across the site. Two occupied the main yard and were boarded up, with a further five spread out in various positions in the field behind. Karen divided the team, so they approached all seven buildings simultaneously. Karen, Jade, Ed, and a uniformed officer headed for the main building as the rest of the team split off.

"I can't see a way of getting in," Jade whispered. She led the way as they circled round the front. It was difficult to see what lay beyond due to the boarded-up windows. Together, they searched all the windows and doors, looking for any visible signs of loosened or dislodged boarding. Other than loads of graffiti sprayed across them and discarded beer cans and wine bottles that lay strewn across the ground, their search threw up nothing.

Karen tapped Jade on the shoulder and pointed towards the smaller of the two buildings. The four of them made their way across the yard before stopping by the doorway. This appeared to be a former farm building split into offices at the front, with its agricultural origins towards the rear. Again, it was impossible for them to see beyond wooden boards that protected the windows and door at the front. As they turned a corner, Karen spotted the rear exit.

Ed checked to see if the board was fixed in place. To his surprise it moved. He placed a finger to his lips and then inched the board away from the rear exit, pausing to take a breath before continuing. It was essential that they gained access to the building without making a noise.

Karen wasn't sure what they would find once they gained entry. The thought crossed her mind that Benton might not be alone, but with four of them, they had a good chance of containing the scene. Karen wasn't prepared to take any chances and sent a text message to other officers on the site to make their way back towards her location.

Ed had created a big enough opening for them to step through into a darkened barn. Karen felt the bumpy concrete floor through her shoes and grabbed her phone from her back pocket, and with the aid of the torch studied their surroundings. Straw littered the floor, old rusty tools hung from one wall, and an enormous engine lay in pieces in the middle of the structure. Karen thought someone had dismantled and never fixed a tractor or truck engine. As they moved round the space, she spotted a faint glow coming from the doorway ahead of them.

They made their way towards the light source, and as they got closer, Karen heard a voice. A familiar voice. Archie Benton. This was it. The four of them gathered in readiness, retrieving their extendable batons.

Karen's pulse throbbed in her ears as her mouth ran dry. Taking long steady breaths, she managed to control her racing heart. Directing her light at the other three officers, she nodded at them. She held up three fingers, and one by one, lowered them. As soon as she curled her thumb in, she pushed through the door. "Police! Don't move!" she shouted. The other officers repeated the warning, their shouts echoed round them.

Archie Benton froze on the spot, his eyes wide with shock. Ed and the uniformed officer raced towards him and dragged him to the ground. It took effort to roll his enormous frame on to his front so they could secure his hands behind his back.

Shock and fear left Karen and Jade paralysed for a moment. What had they walked in on? Tied to a chair by her ankles and wrists, Louisa White's naked and dirty body showed signs of bruising. Her figure sat motionless, her head hung low, her matted and tangled hair dangled and touched her thighs. The chair sat in the middle of a large plastic sheet. A golf club and a knife lay close by. A laptop sat on the table a few feet away, and from it ran leads to several video cameras and tripods positioned at the four corners of the sheets. Two industrial arc lights were set up and the hum of a small generator rumbled in the background. An overwhelming stench of decay, bodily waste, and farmyard smells assaulted their nostrils.

Karen closed her eyes for a second. It felt like they were too late.

Jade ran to Louisa, swept her hair out of the way while lifting the battered woman's chin, and checked for a pulse. "She's alive!"

Karen wanted to cry. She wanted to say something, but her throat choked up as she joined Jade. "You're safe."

"Louisa... Louisa. It's the police. I'm Jade, a police officer. Can you hear me?"

Karen glanced across at Benton, who sat in a seating position with his legs crossed and his arms secured behind him. With his head bowed, Ed arrested him and read Benton his caution. Karen knew what he was thinking as more officers appeared. Desperate to give Louisa some dignity, Karen took off her coat and placed it over the front of Louisa, wrapping it over her bony shoulders.

Reaching for her radio, Karen called control with the good news and requested paramedics and an air ambulance. Louisa needed immediate medical attention. "Jade, help me to cut these cable ties so we can make Louisa more comfortable."

Louisa didn't wince, moan, or open her eyes as they placed her down on the floor and replaced Karen's coat over her.

Karen took a step back to examine the scene. Benton had created a killing room. As she stepped over to the laptop, the genuine horror of the situation surfaced. A stream of messages with vile comments with usernames and no profiles appeared on the screen. Karen shook her head. The messages had stopped at the exact moment they had raided the room. It was a bloody live feed. She grabbed the leads from the laptop and pulled them out but kept the laptop on. Experts from the high-tech unit would need to attend to preserve and capture evidence. Benton was killing his victims with a live audience of anonymous individuals. If that wasn't bad enough, Karen gritted her teeth when she saw a separate window with what appeared to be financial bids. The total stood at $28,332. Shit.

The shock on everyone's faces was palpable as officers stood in silence taking in the macabre scene. Karen had seen nothing like this in her career, nor did she want to see it again. It wasn't long before she heard the whooping sound of helicopter blades above and the sound of approaching sirens.

It saddened her to see Louisa's broken and bruised body. She knelt down and held Louisa's cold and grubby hand. Karen gave it a gentle squeeze, but Louisa didn't respond. She needed a sign, any sign that Louisa could hear. It was hard to know what to say. So much of her wanted to wrap her arms round Louisa and give her the warmth and comfort she needed.

Paramedics arrived moments later, so Karen and Jade

stepped back to allow them to do their work. The officers lifted Benton to his feet and hauled him out of the room, but he still refused to lift his head to look at Louisa or any of the other officers. Bart and his forensic team had now arrived and were getting ready to move in as soon as Louisa was treated and taken to the air ambulance.

Karen reached for her phone and made the call she had waited to make for days. She cleared her throat as another swell of emotion filled her chest.

"Owen, we've found Louisa. She is badly injured, but she is alive." Owen didn't reply for a few seconds and Karen imagined the emotion he felt too, as she heard a loud sniff.

"Jesus, talk about a grown man crying," he muttered.

Karen's eyes moistened again.

"That's good. Fantastic. I'll call Louisa's parents now and we'll make our way over to York. I'll see you later." Owen paused for a moment. "Thank you," he whispered.

54

THE HORROR of what the team had discovered left them shell-shocked. With officers milling round and discussing what may have taken place over recent days, Karen took a few moments to step away to be with her thoughts. They had arrived in the nick of time, and though Louisa's injuries would heal, she wondered if Louisa would ever be the same again. How could anyone recover from such an ordeal? The mental scars would always be there.

One message she had seen on the laptop referred to Louisa sitting in the 'arena'. And as Karen cast her eye round the scene, she understood what that meant. The chair on the plastic sheet, the arc lights, and video cameras that streamed her suffering to a virtual, live audience for their twisted pleasure. *Sick bastards.*

Officers had already checked the three doors leading off the main room. With each open, Karen peered into the first room and hovered by the doorway, not wishing to venture in and contaminate what was in effect a cell and a crime scene. The overwhelming smell of bodily waste soured her taste buds as the smell crept up her nostrils.

She grimaced. The women had been held in this place. There was nothing in there other than a black plastic bucket. The floor was scattered with scraps of green and blue mouldy bread. She shook her head in anger. There was no bedding, not even a blanket. *Clothes?* None to be seen. He'd let them shiver in the midst of winter with no means of keeping warm.

She almost missed it. A small camera suspended from the ceiling with a red flashing light. He was broadcasting their plight when they were at their most vulnerable. Anger boiled inside her. She wanted to rip out Benton's throat. He was an animal.

She visited the other two rooms, and they were the same. Each one identical in shape and size. Each one smelling the same. The conditions were degrading and punishing. SOCO needed to capture all of this so the jury could witness the extent of Archie Benton's evilness. She was sure that Benton would spend the rest of his life in jail, and she looked forward to sitting across the table from him when she interviewed him shortly.

Jade came and stood alongside Karen and peered into the cell. "The air ambulance is taking Louisa to York Hospital. They have alerted the medical staff and I've sent officers to the hospital to give Louisa and her family privacy from prying eyes."

"Karen," an officer called out. "You're needed outside."

Karen turned and walked out to the yard behind the building. Two officers stood round a smouldering oil drum, wispy white plumes of smoke spiralling into the night air.

"You need to look inside," one officer said. He shone his torch into the depths of the steel drum as Karen approached.

The strong odour of burnt plastic filled the air, causing

her eyes to water as she looked inside. Once she'd fanned the worst of the smoke away, she spotted a scattering of teeth, blackened but still identifiable. Judging from the size and shape, she was pretty certain they were human teeth. "Let Bart, the CSI manager, know about this."

"Will do." The officer turned and headed off in search of Bart.

Time wasn't on her side and the clock was ticking. She needed to go back and look into the eyes of Archie Benton.

55

THOUGH ARCHIE BENTON did not resist arrest, his sheer size and presence necessitated the presence of an extra officer standing behind him in the interview suite for added protection. Karen and Ed sat across the table to him. Benton's request for his solicitor to attend, caused a delay of an hour until his brief, Mrs Daria Critchlow, arrived bleary-eyed and wearing a hastily thrown on two-piece suit and blouse.

Each time Karen asked him the usual questions, he responded with no comment. Because he was caught in the act of torturing Louisa White, his brief had little opportunity to defend him. The extra hour waiting for Mrs Critchlow had given Karen and her team a brief opportunity to view video snippets of the attack on Louisa before they'd arrived. They had witnessed him strike her around the body, pausing occasionally to observe the incoming requests from his online viewers. Several of Louisa's teeth had been forcefully removed with pliers against her will, and many of her officers had looked away when they'd heard the spine-tingling screams of pain that Louisa had let out before she'd passed out.

The video footage they'd downloaded on a USB stick also contained disturbing and harrowing images of the last moments of Georgia's and Raveena's lives. With Benton's face in each of the clips, he remained silent as Karen replayed them on a laptop for Benton and Critchlow to see. The sheer barbarity and the harrowing screams which filled the interview room made Critchlow close her eyes and look away.

As Karen stared at the woman, noticing her trembling hands, she wondered if Critchlow could even bring herself to defend the monster.

The one-sided interview continued for more than an hour before Karen sat back in her chair and sighed. It was three a.m.. She'd been awake for nearly twenty-four hours and despite having pulled many all-nighters in her career, the sweltering and stuffy environment in the room, the absence of sleep and food, and the lack of progress in the interview, left her completely drained and fatigued. Ed didn't seem much better either as she glanced at him and noticed the lattice of red veins in his eyes.

"Is there anything you want to say?" Karen said.

"No comment."

"Do you feel any remorse or guilt for what you have done to these three women?"

"No comment."

"Did you for one minute think of the devastation that you have caused to two families who have lost their daughters, and the third family who face years of trying to rebuild their lives?"

"No comment."

The man infuriated her. He was a walking embodiment of filth, rudeness, and cruelty. He entertained his own twisted fantasies in exchange for a financial reward, and as she stared at him, he showed no sign of remorse.

Karen closed her folder and terminated the interview. She waited for Ed to switch off the recorder before taking one last look at Benton. "I hope you think this was worth it, because you'll be spending the rest of your life in a cell half the size of what you put Georgia, Raveena, and Louisa in. And I suspect that you'll be looking over your shoulder in prison every single day because you have a target on your back, and I don't think you'll get another night of restful sleep for as long as you live." Karen leant into the table. "And you deserve everything that is coming your way."

"Take him back to his cell," Ed told the officer.

KAREN RETURNED to her office and flopped down in her chair, her arms dangled on either side of the armrests. She wanted to sleep for a week, but there was so much to do. The case had been put forward to the CPS, and now they waited for a charging decision. Her eyes felt so heavy, and she'd lost count of the number of black coffees she'd consumed since coming back to the station.

"Ah, there you are." Kelly appeared in Karen's doorway, wearing a Nike hoodie, dark blue jeans, and a pair of trainers.

Karen sat straight up, astonished at the sight of the super. "Ma'am, I wasn't expecting you."

Kelly ran a hand through her hair and yawned. "Neither was I, but I got a call from the CC."

The case had been a high-profile investigation from the offset, and with so many forces involved across the country, she wasn't surprised the CC had called Kelly.

"How did you get on with the interview?"

"The usual, ma'am. Unwilling to cooperate and a load of no comments. It doesn't matter. The evidence is compelling. We've caught him in the act. A ton of physical evidence, and what appears to be hours of footage of him torturing and killing Georgia and Raveena, and in the process of killing Louisa. I'm just waiting for the CPS decision. I'm hoping for three counts of abduction and imprisonment, two murders, and one attempted murder."

"Well done to you and the team. Get the charging decision and then go home. We need him remanded in custody."

"Absolutely," Karen said. She yawned and rubbed her eyes. "I can't go home yet. I need to head to the hospital. Owen is bringing Louisa's parents over now. They should be there shortly. I'd like to be there to see them and answer any questions they may have."

"There's no need. I can arrange for them to be put up in a hotel after they've seen Louisa, and you can see them tomorrow."

"I know, ma'am. But I'd like to."

Kelly shrugged. "Okay. It's a nice gesture on our part. Make sure you thank the DCI for his help at their end. I'm going to head home now. I've got a debrief with the CC in six hours."

Karen watched Kelly head off down the corridor. She dragged her weary body out of the chair, grabbed the car keys, handbag, and coat, and headed for the hospital.

56

ONE WEEK LATER.

The smell of hospital disinfectant surrounded her as Karen made her way to Louisa White's ward. She had visited Louisa and her parents several times over the last few days, not only to check up on Louisa and ensure she was okay, but also to update her parents, Michael and Alison, on the preparation of the case file for a future court date.

So much had happened in the last seven days. They'd discovered further bone and teeth fragments in the oil drum. Benton had made efforts to eliminate the evidence, but fragments still existed and were a DNA match for Georgia and Raveena. In addition, the investigators had discovered traces of the women's DNA in the nose of the pliers and the face of a golf club lying close by at the scene. The presence of Benton's DNA on both the pliers and golf club had provided further compelling evidence that sealed his fate.

This case was a collaborative effort by teams both locally and nationally.

Bart's team had played a crucial role in gathering the evidence against Benton. Without the usual help from CCTV, Karen had relied on forensic evidence, right down to the pollen spores found on Georgia which were a compositional match to scrapings taken from the barn.

The forensic high-tech unit were working with their National Crime Agency and the European and international counterparts to uncover the identities behind the usernames who had taken part in the online bidding. Their work would take weeks, months, or years, but they were determined to bring them to justice.

Karen stopped outside the ward and applied hand sanitiser from the dispenser. She smiled when she thought of Jade who would no doubt have drained the contents by now.

A room off the main corridor was provided for Louisa so that she could rest and recover away from the glare of others on the ward. She looked so young and broken as Karen stood in the doorway. Michael and Alison sat on either side of the bed, watching their daughter as she slept. Having spoken to the doctors, Karen knew that Louisa had suffered no long-lasting internal injuries, and it would take a few weeks for the bruising round her face, chest, and arms to heal. She would also need dental work in the future to replace her missing teeth.

Physically, Louisa had been lucky. But it was her mental state that concerned doctors. She woke many times with nightmares, and for the majority of her time there, she stayed asleep, waking only to gaze at the ceiling in a near catatonic state. Her parents hadn't been able to get a word out of her.

Alison White looked over her shoulder and saw Karen. She rose from her chair and stepped out into the corridor.

"How is Louisa?"

Alison sighed. Tears filled her eyes. "We don't know. We've got our daughter back, but we don't know how much of our daughter is still there."

Karen pulled her into an embrace as Alison sobbed. She offered words of reassurance. "It will take time. Time for her to process what's happened, and lots of love and support from her friends and family. The hospital will arrange for professional help, but for now, she needs her mum and dad beside her." Karen experienced the emotion building in her chest, and sensed their pain, anguish, and helplessness. Louisa White was a twenty-year-old young woman. To her parents, she was still their little girl.

"You've got my number if you need anything. Between Swansea police and me, we'll keep in touch."

Alison wiped her tears away with the back of her hand. "Thank you. Thank you for everything you did to save our Louisa. Will you be attending Georgia's and Raveena's funerals?"

Karen nodded. "We'll be there." She watched as Alison turned and went back in to take a seat beside her daughter.

The chilly night air gripped her lungs as Karen stepped out into the darkness and walked back to her car. She needed time to process the case in much the same way that Michael and Alison did. Reaching into her handbag, Karen grabbed the car keys, unlocked the door and slid into her seat. She was about to start the car when her phone rang. It was an unidentified number. She frowned and answered it.

"Hello?" No-one replied, but she heard the faint sound of breathing at the other end. "Hello? Who is this?"

The line went dead.

She was too tired to think about the caller as she tossed her phone back into her bag and headed home.

CURRENT BOOK LIST

Hop over to my website for a current list of books:
http://jaynadal.com/current-books/

OTHER WAYS TO STAY IN TOUCH

Other ways you can connect with me:

Like my page on Facebook: Jay Nadal

Email jay@jaynadal.com with any questions, ideas or interesting story suggestions. Hey, even if you spot a typo that we've missed, then drop me a line!

ABOUT THE AUTHOR

Author of:

The DI Scott Baker Crime Series
The DI Karen Heath Crime Series
The Thomas Cade PI Series

Printed in Great Britain
by Amazon